Additional Praise for

FOOLS

"The linked characters in Joan Silber's collection *Fools* . . . go from the fiercely principled (young anarchists in 1920s Greenwich Village) to the fervently hedonistic (a newly married hotelier's son who can't resist temptation). But it's those who admit their ambivalence—such as the daughter of a conscientious objector whose life detours from the wifely domesticity she envisioned—who approach true dissidence." —*Vogue*

"Elegant. . . . Timely." —*Village Voice*

"A memorable meditation on work, religion, love, and the search for personal integrity." —*Booklist*, starred review

"Powerful and moving. . . . Recalls Jennifer Egan's *A Visit from the Goon Squad* in its novelistic cohesion of multiple sprawling tales." —*Library Journal*, starred review

"Joan Silber's stories are like compressed novels. They are interlocking tales that fill in the history of revolutionary politics in the twentieth century." —Edmund White

"*Fools* is astonishing for its range, for its sweeping sense of time and place, and most especially for its deep insight into the way small choices can circle out to shape lives, and even human history. This is a beautiful book and an important literary achievement." —Dan Chaon

"Joan Silber's stories charm us. And amuse us. And engage us. And move us. And even enlighten us. *Fools* embraces us all."

—Amy Bloom

"Joan Silber is one of the wisest, finest, most capacious observers of the human condition writing now. We should all be as heartbreakingly foolish and beautiful as the characters in this collection. Silber understands them inside out, and brings them close to us, as no one else can."

—Stacey D'Erasmo

"*Fools* is a unique and fascinating collection that celebrates not so much a place or a family or a single life as it does an idea—anarchy—as it runs through three generations of loosely connected people. The collective vision this provokes is what makes the book intellectually satisfying; the separate lives it convincingly displays are what move the heart."

—Antonya Nelson

"In Joan Silber's dazzling new story collection, written in elegant prose and with clairvoyant wisdom, the loves and aspirations, both spiritual and material, of six very different people reaffirm in unexpected ways the fallibility and the essential sameness of our human condition."

—Lily Tuck

"*Fools* is a wonderfully winning exploration of impetuousness in all of its appalling and appealing forms, and its deftly interconnected stories are devoted to those dreamers who act rashly out of their better natures, who never quit asking the world *Can't you do better than that?*—a question certain to become increasingly urgent as this twenty-first century progresses."

—Jim Shepard

"*Fools* is great fiction. Here are anarchists and pacifists, protesters in causes to do with freedom and equality, causes to which these self-aware men and women devote themselves—or not. It is impossible not to be enthralled." —Christine Schutt

"I loved *Fools*. The stories always surprised me, with the narratives unfolding as if in real time, and then turning unexpected in so many ways, twisting into stories that felt like remembered history, but with such added emotion that I thought about the characters for several days afterward as if they were here in my house." —Susan Straight

FOOLS

JOAN SILBER

W. W. Norton & Company
NEW YORK • LONDON

For Chuck Wachtel

For information about permission to reproduce
selections from this book,
write to Permissions, W. W. Norton & Company, Inc.,
500 Fifth Avenue, New York, NY 10110

For information about special discounts for bulk purchases,
please contact W. W. Norton Special Sales at
specialsales@wwnorton.com or 800-233-4830

Manufacturing by Courier Westford
Book design by Brooke Koven
Production manager: Devon Zahn

Library of Congress Cataloging-in-Publication Data

Silber, Joan.
[Short stories. Selections]
Fools / Joan Silber. — First edition.
pages cm
ISBN 978-0-393-08870-0 (hardcover)
I. Title.
PS3569.I414F66 2013
813'.54—dc23

2013000342

ISBN 978-0-393-34889-7 pbk.

W. W. Norton & Company, Inc.
500 Fifth Avenue, New York, N.Y. 10110
www.wwnorton.com

W. W. Norton & Company Ltd.
Castle House, 75/76 Wells Street, London W1T 3QT

1 2 3 4 5 6 7 8 9 0

ACKNOWLEDGMENTS

For their good advice and great generosity, I want to thank Andrea Barrett, Myra Goldberg, Kathleen Hill, Margot Livesey, and Chuck Wachtel. I am grateful, as ever, to my agent, Geri Thoma, and to my new editor, Jill Bialosky. For their helpful conversation, a thank you to Elspeth Leacock and Claudia Leacock. Special thanks once again to Sharon Captan for her friendship.

The story "Fools" appeared previously in *Northwest Review*, "Two Opinions" and "Better" appeared in *Epoch*, and "Buying and Selling" appeared in *Agni*. "Two Opinions" is included in *The PEN/O. Henry Prize Stories 2012*. "Fools" is included in *New America: Contemporary Literature for a Changing Society*, ed. Holly Messitt and James Tolan (Autumn House, 2013).

CONTENTS

If the fool would persist in his folly he would become wise.

—WILLIAM BLAKE

I am painfully aware of the fact that conduct everywhere falls far short of belief.

—MOHANDAS K. GANDHI

Happiness is when what you think, what you say, and what you do are in harmony.

—MOHANDAS K. GANDHI

Our problems stem from our acceptance of this filthy, rotten system.

—DOROTHY DAY

FOOLS

Fools

A lot of people thought anarchists were fools. I finished high school in 1924, and even during my girlhood, when the fiercest wing of anarchists still believed in "propaganda by deed" and threw bombs and shot at world leaders, people thought they did it out of a bloody kind of sappiness, a laughable naïveté. All this laughing, I came to think, ignored the number of things a person could be a fool for in this life—a fool for love, a fool for Christ, a fool for admiration. I had friends who were all of these, as it turned out. But I took my own route.

I wasn't born into anarchism. I read myself into it. Someone handed me a pamphlet in the street, and that was the beginning. And my cousin Joe was an influence. Joe was a third cousin, hardly related at all, but in our teen years we were both enlisted in my mother's brief attempt to distribute used clothes to the poor in our church. Musty woolen topcoats, faded school pinafores, piles and piles of men's hats. The problem was, my mother was afraid of the people who showed up for the clothes. We stood behind a table in the dank church basement while she pled for an orderly line and whispered at me not to touch the children. On the other side, Joe was muttering to me about why we had these extra goods and they didn't.

I was born in India, in the city of Madras in the state of Tamil Nadu, when my father was a missionary for the Congregationalist Church. We went home to Philadelphia when I was six, but I had memories. My father left the mission in a state of great disillusion, embittered by ecclesiastical infighting in a country so filled with suffering. In America, I was mocked for the way my speech sounded Indian and was hounded in school by a group of bullying girls.

In my adult life, when my friends heard I came from a missionary family, they teased me about how I naturally came from a long line of zealots, didn't I, which was how I liked to view it. Actually, the zealotry had drained by the time I was growing up. My father was just another bald, tired minister who mumbled through the services and didn't really want to look anyone in the eye. My mother was more ardent, more desperate.

I hated the unbearable Ladies' Aid meetings in our living room and the tedious Sunday school with my poor mother teaching improbable platitudes. In high school I was infamous for cynical jokes about the Virgin Mary. Only Joe was worse. In the school auditorium, he passed me notes parodying the psalm read in assembly. (*He that hath clean hands and a pure heart and always washes with Boraxo.*)

When I was reading the books Joe lent me, I felt a kind of joyous relief, once I got past the hard parts. What I loved in anarchism, from the first, was the obvious truth in it: people had gotten it all wrong to expect justice from any state. Power never protected the weak, it only protected itself. Tyranny was built into the system. The clarity of this argument was pretty stunning, I thought, and so was its insistence that this didn't have to continue, despite its long human history.

I was a girl Joe had always known. It hadn't occurred to him to be attracted in a noncousinly way until he saw me in the park one chilly autumn day, listening to speakers for Sacco and Vanzetti. I was leaning against an elm tree when he came striding toward me, with his slicked-back hair and his long-legged walk.

"They think I'm off studying in the library," I said.

"Well, you are, Vera."

"I've been here awhile," I said. "Aren't you cold? I'm freezing." I shivered for effect, put my hand on his cheek so he could feel its coolness. I knew what I was doing.

I'd had a crush on him for a while. He took off his muffler and wrapped it around my shoulders, coming closer to knot it for me. "Is that better?" he said. How easy this part was.

• • •

All our excited feelings for each other were mixed up with ideas, with anger and vision, but what was wrong with that? Our meandering conversations, full of half-remembered reading and sudden bits of clarity, felt majestic. Together we picketed a textile mill with the workers—on a Saturday afternoon when my parents thought we were at the pictures, we took a streetcar and then we lined up with a big group. Joe was a fast walker and we were up in the front with the yelling schoolboys. I kept close to Joe, I heard myself yell and chant. It was my first time in public as this form of myself.

Joe was older than I was, by a year. Once he was done with high school, he got a managing job in a printing office. He liked being out in the world, and all the mechanical processes of rotary presses and dry offset were interesting enough to him, but he had to put in very long hours. And I had a baby brother I took care of. On Saturdays I'd take my fat little Robert to the park in his carriage, and Joe would walk the paths with us, wheeling the carriage for me, so I could take his arm.

My mother spoke of us as courting, but this was a mis-understanding on her part. We didn't mean to marry at all. We both assumed we would be together for life, no papers needed. I really loved that idea—the purity of our bond, without the government having anything to say about it or any religious body presuming it could sanctify us. The whole notion of a legal wedding seemed profoundly disrespectful to us, us of all people. I was so insulted when my sister said, "What's to keep Joe from taking off? He could go anytime. You want that?" No one believed how unfair that was to Joe or how belittling to me.

We were still at home with our families, and we didn't hide our plans, we were nothing if not straightforward. My parents were not backward or strict, as clerical families went. They didn't send me away to a distant relative, they didn't lock me in my bedroom. But they wouldn't let Joe in our house again. No matter how many times he came to the door. My mother told me, "You think we could ever get over it if you did this? We never would." My father said, "There's a reason for the commandments. Don't you feel God all around you? You think you're above God?"

Outrage might just have hardened us, if there hadn't also been tears. I heard my father weeping! My tired, desiccated father. It was a choked, unnatural, gasping sound through the wall. What were we doing, Joe and I? I began to think we were sticking too blindly to a technical point. Like my friend Mary Elizabeth from grade school, who thought eating a raisin before going to Communion was wrong. One raisin. Who cared, what did it matter, if we said a few words in a public ceremony? Was cruelty better? Even Joe agreed, though his face had a terrible half-smile of embarrassment. It hurt us to have me see him. So, in the end, we were hypocrites for kindness. Both of us. Standing with my bouquet of orange blossoms, I thought: *I'm happy but I'm in disguise.* But probably many people feel that at their weddings.

• • •

We lived for two months in an apartment overlooking a box factory, and then, as soon as we could, we moved from the Philadelphia of our families to the freer, more unknown spaces of New York. First we were in a very cramped and desolate room in a boardinghouse, and then, after we started going to meetings and had more of a social life, we shared a place in the Village with a couple named Betsy and Norman and a single man named Richard and his dog, Bakunin. Sometimes other people too. I liked this arrangement very well.

We didn't drink as much as the others, but we didn't seem to need to—we got into the arguing and the clowning and the repudiating of theories at just as high a volume without it. We were testing how to be right. Richard was the most dogged in posing questions.

"Joe," he would say, "what would you do if you caught a man stealing your wallet? Would you have him arrested?"

Joe was against prisons, we all were. Kropotkin had called them "universities of crime." "I'd grab my wallet and really talk to him," Joe said.

"Oh, that talk," Betsy said. "Maybe he'd rather be in jail."

But I thought it was a good answer.

I brought up Tolstoy's hero in *Resurrection*, who decided prisons had never, ever done any good. "Listen to her," Joe said. "Are you listening?" Everyone knew I'd read more than Betsy.

"Tolstoy said money was a new form of slavery," I said. "People don't read his essays."

"Only *you* have set eyes on them, I guess," Richard said. "Don't brag, it's never effective." This embarrassed me and I really did stop bragging after that.

Dorothy, a friend of Richard's who liked to drink with us, said, "I've been in jail. It didn't reform me." She was in her late twenties, older than we were, and she'd once been arrested in a march for women's suffrage. And now she never voted, because she'd come to believe that voting was colluding. I admired these scruples.

I liked watching Joe when he waited to speak, his solid chin, his dark, soft eyes. My mother had told me that the first years of her marriage were the hardest ones, but the shock of cohabitation went fine for us, mostly. We had the fire and puzzle of ideas, a goad to keep our better selves showing. And we had all those other people around.

None of us slept enough. The others went out after midnight to drink at a speakeasy a few blocks away. They had less regular jobs, looser hours—they wrote articles for magazines, they sketched ladies' fashions for department store ads, and I thought Betsy had money from her family. Joe had found work in a print shop uptown, and I had a job painting letters for a sign and banner place in the neighborhood. I had always liked to draw and sketch and used to do all the decorating in the church.

This was a very good time for us. Joe loved the long debates, but at the end of any evening, once we were in our room, he would say, "I am *so* tired," and make a big joke of collapsing against me, where lust took over whatever fatigue either of us had. How luxuriant those nights were, our secret lives of excess.

• • •

We'd come to the city in the thick heat of late summer, but within a month we were in an autumn of clear days, of morning air with light in every molecule. I made a vow to walk to my job, to get more time in the sudden freshness outside, but this excellent habit lasted two days. I envied our friend Dorothy, who owned a tiny, unheated bungalow by the beach in Staten Island. A very nice man named Forster stayed with her there on weekends, when he wasn't working in the city. They claimed to live on bootleg wine and the fish he caught. Once they brought us a basket of lovely shells that smelled like drying seaweed and I put the shells all around our room, big white whelks and nacreous jingle shells, thin as paper, and blue cockles striped with yellow, on the mantel and the bed table. "Think of this as your island hideaway," I said to Joe, as I flipped down the covers. "Where the roaring surf echoes the passion of mortals."

"I hear it, I hear it," Joe said.

Joe had never been to the ocean, but I had. My mother walked with me along the Jersey shore when she was trying to talk me into giving up Joe. I was busy thinking at that moment how the rhythm of the surf sounded like a great animal breathing, sounded like the pulse of sex. I knew what sex was, or thought I did—my mind was entirely colored by the few chances Joe and I had taken. I sat with my mother on a bench along the sands, watching the curling froth and trough of the waves, and I had remembrances that made me feel smug in her company.

"We can take the ferry to Coney Island sometime," Joe said, taking off his shoes.

"This is our island," I said to Joe, setting my palm on the bed.

Joe liked this sort of beckoning frankness. (He was reaching for me now, while he turned down the lamp with his other hand.) As long as it wasn't too frank. If my praise of his body ran to candid exactness, if I was moved to use blunt and stumbling language to exalt something we'd done, he would laugh and say, "Yes, yes," but not happily. So I stopped doing that. Everyone thought Joe was the bolder of us, but no one knows how a couple fits together. The twists in that knot. For his part, Joe had learned not to talk so much when we were already lying in bed at night, not to squander this time reflecting on his day until we were too sleepy for love. The quarrels we had turned each of us huffy but caused useful corrections.

Dorothy had said that their beach was glorious at night, with tall, skinny pines against the sky and lights in the houses along the shore and the rolling surf invisible and tremendous in the dark, and I was thinking of that now, while Joe and I entered our own night, our own sea. We stayed awake so long we could hear the clop of the horse's hooves outside when the milk truck went by in the very early morning.

In the morning, when Joe and I got up, only the dog—a big mongrel with some police dog in him—was awake and pacing the kitchen. The others always slept late. But I sort of liked being someone who went to work, and I didn't mind my job. Nothing fascinating, but I could lose myself in it.

I spent a perfectly pleasant afternoon painting—in dark brown and ivy-green—a sign that suggested to all passersby

ADAMS CHICLETS
"Genuinely and Truly Delightful to All"

with a spearmint leaf below. The leaf was easy and I took pride in adding serrated edges, tiny veins, a jaunty stem.

It was true that chewing gum was a worthless product, a clever vendor's dream of packaged nothing. Betsy refused to buy it. My father had banned chewing gum for all his daughters, who were not to be seen masticating like cows. My poor father. In India the people used to chew *beeda* after a meal, to freshen the mouth and aid digestion—a leaf with sweet spices rolled into it. My mother was in anguish, close to tears, when men spit its red juice in the street.

My unhappy mother. What an effort she always strove to make. Sometimes now she wrote me letters. *Regards to my dearest son-in-law. I hope that he is enjoying your cooking!* She would never really like Joe, never forgive him for wanting to dishonor me. I made fun of her letters to my friends, as if I were the sort of person who wanted a bluffer, franker mother.

When I finished the sign, my boss, Mr. Frances, said, "The leaf looks like a caterpillar somebody stepped on."

"It's mint," I said. "We used to grow it in our yard."

"Do I pay you to be an imbecile?" Mr. Frances said. "I'm the imbecile then, aren't I?" He talked to all of us like that.

Sometimes he docked our pay when he didn't like the way

the signs turned out. Ten cents, or even twenty cents, enough for a meal. He called it fining us for artistic offenses. Or he'd have us stay late into the night to paint a sign over again. "Right is right," he'd say. A few times I'd passed out union literature to try to organize our little group of workers, but that was as far as my bravery went.

"You're one of the sloppiest, least talented sign-painters I've had the misfortune to be around," Mr. Frances said, "and anyone can see it. Isn't that true?"

That was the worst, his wanting you to agree. He always wanted that.

"I don't know," I said.

"Yes, you do," Mr. Frances said.

I took my brushes to the sink to soak them in a jar of turpentine. "You do know," he said.

I had the water running, and I kept my back to him. I didn't want to look for another job. We had no savings.

"You do know," Mr. Frances said.

The others had stopped talking. I wiped my hands on the towel. I should have turned around but I didn't. The room was waiting.

"I know," I said.

What if he fired me anyway? They were looking at me, the others, but they all would have done the same thing.

"Go home to your husband who has to put up with you," Mr. Frances said.

I put on my jacket and got out of there. I thought about Joe the whole walk home. In my head I was explaining, trying to make myself sound better. Most of my days were not as bad as this one, but the sweetness and the one true thing at the end of all of them was Joe.

I didn't stop to say anything to the others when I came in the door. I went down the hall at once to change out of the clothes that smelled of turpentine. I waited, sitting on the bed, and when Joe came in, tired and inky himself, he had to hear about my day.

"It's not for *profit* that the man acts that way," I said. "It's to push someone around. He can't resist. Do you think that's a human instinct?"

"Of course," Joe said. "But we overcome other instincts. We're housebroken, we don't go around mounting each other's wives."

I had to go in to work the next day too. Joe had his hand on my knee as we spoke. I leaned against him, against the hard span of his chest. "I've compromised too much, haven't I?" I said. "It's ugly."

But I was as blithe as anyone when Betsy decided later that night that we should all go out to a speakeasy she liked. There I was, only hours after my unspeakable day, singing "Beautiful Dreamer" with her at the bar. She had a better voice than I did but I could keep on key after drinking. "Out on the sea," I sang, "mermaids are chanting the wild lorelie."

I secretly loved the song. Joe and Forster were talking nearby—Forster kept saying Goya was the best draftsman who ever lived. "No! Rembrandt!" I said. Gin makes you very certain about things. I didn't want to fight with Forster or cross him. "I really like Rembrandt," I said, more quietly and dumbly.

Dorothy said, "Nobody ever gets over those Goya war etchings. It's Goya."

"What about the leper?" I said. "What about what Rembrandt does with Christ healing the leper?"

"You people," Betsy said, "have such grim ideas of beauty."

"Beautiful dreamers," Joe said. "What queens of song you are."

"I bet you can sing," Betsy said. "Can you sing?"

"Like a half-dead frog."

"Frogs have outstanding voices," Dorothy said. "As good as crickets."

I thought they all liked Joe better than me. *I* liked Joe better than me. He was a better talker, more showy and funny, and also more uniformly nice. Now he was twanging a frog's version of "Beautiful Dreamer" and then "Swanee River." Did Dorothy fancy him? Probably not. She could sometimes flirt but she loved Forster.

"Some frogs can inflate their throats to the size of their heads," Forster said.

"Only you would know that," I said.

After Christmas, when the weather turned bitter cold, I was the one who ended up walking the dog when Richard didn't want to bother going out, and I often ran into Forster in Washington Square. He had a favorite bench by the ginkgo trees on the south side. Like the dog, he liked to be outside.

"You're not cold sitting there?" I said. Bakunin the dog was investigating Forster's shoes. It was a Sunday morning and not very many humans were out.

"I don't mind," he said. "Dorothy says I just don't notice."

"In Tibet there are lamas who sit out naked in winter," I said. "They slow themselves down, I think."

"I'm afraid I'm not a lama," he said.

"Fine with me," I said. "I'm not disappointed."

Forster smiled faintly at this. He was quieter than the others; you had to work to talk to him. "I've had enough clergy in my life," I said.

"Dorothy has quite a religious side," he said. "I have to say, it's superstition to me."

Bakunin barked at a squirrel, and I let him off the leash. He never caught any but it made him feel important to chase. We watched him leap at a sycamore, surprised each time that he couldn't get up the tree by jumping. He consoled himself by sniffing at a man sleeping on a bench nearby. "Bakunin!" I said. "Don't bother that person."

The dog was whining. "No," I said. "He's not waking up to play with you." A howling wail came out of the dog, a sound I had not heard him make before—a siren with a long quaver. Or was it the man howling? It wasn't the man. He wasn't moving. He was probably too cold to move.

"I'll get Bakunin," Forster said.

I went with him. The man on the bench had rolled himself in a filthy overcoat and pulled the top of it over his head. He was lying sideways on the bench, with his feet jutting off the edge—bare feet, grayed with dirt. What kind of city lets a man go shoeless in ten-degree weather? Even the cracked skin on the ankles looked like stone, not skin. Forster touched the man's shoulder (very kindly, I thought) and said, "Sorry, sorry."

I almost said, *What an argument against alcohol!* but it wasn't a joke I wanted the man to hear. Anyone sleeping outside in winter was beyond desperate. Forster was bent over him, peering at whatever bit of the face showed from under the coat.

"Will you stay here," Forster said, "while I try to find a policeman?"

"He's not all right?" I said.

"No," Forster said. "He can't hurt you, don't worry."

I looked at the face myself. The helpless mouth, the empty eyes. When you grow up in the parish house of a church, you know what dead people look like. I gave a small, useless shriek, and then I said, "Go now."

Once Forster was gone, I became alarmed that he hadn't checked the man over more closely. What if the man was only sick and frozen, and there was something I should be doing? I started to rub his bare feet, to chafe them into warming. They were stiff under my gloves, but feet are always stiff. It was horrible to think I was bothering a dead man with my touch, but I kept it up. I thought of Dorothy, who'd trained as a nurse during the war and might've known what to do.

I said, "It's all right, it's all right," to the body. The head had lank hair and a broken tooth showing from under the lip. I had to stay where Forster had left me, but I was afraid of the man as a corpse and afraid of him as a live human who might wake up dangerous. And then I was ashamed to be so interested in my own *feelings* when I was standing over a man at the border of life.

And the feet. I wouldn't let the dog sniff them, I pushed his muzzle away. I knew perfectly well that they were Christ's feet, even though I no longer took any of that literally. How could I not know? I was still chanting, "It's all right," and rubbing the shoeless feet, when Forster got there with a policeman.

"Please hold the dog, miss," the cop said. Then he did all the things Forster and I should have done. He cupped his palm under the nostrils to feel for warm breath, he clasped the wrist where the pulse would be, he reached under the man's shirt to find his heart.

"It's bad?" Forster said.

"Bad as it gets," he said. "You can go. Thank you. Thank you very much."

I was going to say, *Rest his soul*, but I didn't, because I didn't want Forster to think I was a ninny. I followed him on the path.

"Doesn't it seem very noisy outside, all of a sudden?" I said. "We've been elsewhere."

"Yes," Forster said. "I'm not quite back yet."

We were at the edge of the park, in the cold. Everything was too vivid, after our time spent guessing how far the man was from anything we knew. The bare quiet was still in our heads. We walked without speaking—I was glad of that. How tinny and insubstantial everything in the shop windows was, how childish. What did anyone need a feather-topped hat for?

In front of my building, Forster said, "Go sit by yourself somewhere, if you can."

"I wish we'd been there sooner for him," I said.

"That part makes me furious," he said. "No one cares about a man like that."

He put his hand on my shoulder. I was afraid to touch him, with my gloves that had touched the dead man's feet, but I leaned my head slightly.

A few days later, Dorothy told me she'd been saying prayers for the man's soul.

"What kind of prayers?" I said.

We were in the corner of a loud and pleasantly crowded living room where a party was going on. Dorothy had a cigarette in her hand. "To beg that he's taken into heaven. What else can be asked for? And I gave something to the priest at St. Guadeloupe to have him included in their prayers."

Dorothy, poor as a church mouse, was giving coins for this?

"We all had lots of training young, didn't we?" I said.

"Actually, I didn't," she said. "I just like to go into churches, I have for years. Mostly Catholic ones. Especially late at night, after I've been out, I like to go in and see the lit candles. But not only then. And I notice that I tend to pray in my head. Don't ask me Who's listening. I don't have a final opinion."

All this was a surprise. I wasn't one of those who thought that praying was demented—my family prayed pretty constantly—but I thought of myself as done with such things. In Philadelphia I'd gone to meetings (and marched too) with workers whose pamphlets said, "Jesus Saves the Slave," not to mention "Trust in the Lord and Sleep in the Street." Dorothy must've known those lines. She made a living of sorts as a writer and she'd done reporting for radical magazines for years.

"People are at their best when they're in devotion," Dorothy said. "Sometimes I just walk from the beach into town with my rosary beads in my pocket. I don't think it matters if I don't say the words completely right."

Is she unbalanced? I thought. And I saw that I wanted her to be. I had an oddly happy feeling at the thought that she might be not right at all for Forster. I knew what this thought meant. (And didn't I have a husband I loved? I did.) It was my own business what I thought. Not every involuntary wish had to be acted on. *Thoughts are free*, I thought. This was the refrain of a German song they sang at meetings: No man can deny, *Die Gedanken sind frei.*

Dorothy was fishing a piece of fruit out of her empty glass of rum punch. It was the made-up, improvised nature of Dorothy's praying that gave it a semi-crazy taint. And then I was embarrassed to think that. Dorothy was a sensible and highly original person. If she wanted to walk around mentally intoning addresses to pure space, that was her own business, her own liberty.

At the party, someone put on a record of "My Baby Just Cares for Me" and Joe came to claim me for a light, not too bouncy fox trot. Forster wasn't around (he didn't like parties) and Dorothy found Richard to dance with. She talked while she danced, in that smoky room, with her shining cropped hair showing wispy in the light, and she looked like any of us, nicely in rhythm, set on what she was doing, pretty enough.

• • •

Could someone who loved freedom above all believe in a fat, overconstructed, historically corrupt institution like the Catholic Church? Joe and I had several talks about this. Dorothy wasn't even born a Catholic, but if it was truly and freely in her own individual nature to love the Church, what then? "It's the *illusion* in it that gives me the creeps," Joe said. He meant divinity. Christ's or anybody's. Couldn't you be opposed to submission—I didn't expect to ever again kneel to pray—but be receptive to what Dorothy liked to call the Unseen? "Not possible, I don't think," Joe said. "Name me a religion where people don't bow their heads."

I wasn't keen to think about it, now that I was away from my father's house. I didn't need to have an opinion, in the life I had. But I saw how lit up Dorothy was, how charged with bits of liturgy, how stirred and driven, how thirsty. She would start to find us all shallow, if she kept on this way. But we had our own beliefs, our hopes for knocking down the stupidities of the past. "She thinks we're nothing," Joe said.

"Don't be vain about it," I said. "That is not the problem." But I was hurt too, that Dorothy could think of leaving us.

Joe and I kept meaning to visit Dorothy's little house in Staten Island, but we didn't get there till the height of summer, when Manhattan was an oven and the beach was fresh and astounding. We all ran around in the surf in our bathing costumes, shrieking when the waves hit us. Forster was out fishing when we got there, but Dorothy's twelve-year-old brother John, who was staying with them, dove fearlessly under the waves and kept teasing his sister by popping up right under where she was. Joe pretended to rescue her by dragging her off. "All the Day family are good swimmers," she said, kicking and escaping. I didn't know then that Dorothy was pregnant.

She was perfectly slender in her sleeveless tunic and narrow swimsuit. I was shorter and rounder and felt more exposed and fleshy, though I forgot myself because of the ease everyone else had. We dried ourselves sitting on the porch, eating blackberries from the garden. The house itself was a mess of specimens that Forster had dragged in—skate egg cases, the skulls of small animals, bird's nests, the shell of a huge turtle—and the kitchen table was piled with pages of a serial romance Dorothy was writing for a newspaper. I envied their lives in that little house.

Forster showed up in time for supper, tanned and wild-haired from the boat and quiet as ever. He had caught a dog-fish, which looked like a small shark—Dorothy said no one around there ate them but an Italian neighbor had said Italians thought they were delicious. So Dorothy fried up pieces in butter and we had potatoes and cabbage salad with them. The fish was strong-tasting but not bad. "Oh," Forster said, "I just had to cut away the venomous part when I filleted it." I thought he was kidding but he wasn't.

"Vera, honey bun, don't be nervous," Joe said, so I decided not to be. Everyone thought Forster knew what he was doing, and I probably thought so too. They lived on nothing, he and Dorothy, and looked better and healthier than the rest of us.

Dorothy told me the news when we were cleaning up in the kitchen. "Don't you notice how magnificent I am?" she said. "It's the end of the second month already. Every morning I give thanks."

I knew she'd had an abortion when she was younger and had suffered for it. And the man had left her afterward. It wasn't much of a secret. A novel she'd written about it had actually been published—*The Eleventh Virgin*, by Dorothy Day—and movie rights had paid for the beach shack, though no one made any such movie. Dorothy was so earnest she didn't bother to have what would be secrets for anyone else.

"I thought Forster was looking very tickled," I said. "Now I get it."

"Forster will get used to the idea," she said. "He thinks it's a terrible world and we shouldn't add to its numbers."

"It is a terrible world," I said, "but he'll be fine."

I meant that he would stick by her. Dorothy didn't appear to doubt this either. She was twenty-eight already.

"He'll teach the baby how to fish," I said. "You'll have the only infant who knows how to surf-cast."

I didn't say it, but I was ever so slightly sorry for Forster, who'd been outmaneuvered, caught off guard. Nature's dupe. He really did only want a few simple things—a life with lots of empty space in it—and now he was getting more than he'd bargained for.

But you always did, in a couple. That was what I thought when I lay next to Joe in the tiny bedroom at the end of the hall. Joe was talking on about how fishermen never had to punch a time clock, no wonder Forster liked it. That was how come Vanzetti had no proof he was at work the night of the Braintree robbery, he was out selling fish. Could he get a lobster to testify he never fired a shot? An eel to swear for him?

It was okay. I might've had a husband who talked about things I cared far less about. "It's so quiet here at night," Joe said. "At home our streets are teeming, aren't they?"

"Most streets," I said.

"And heartless. We're as bad as India," Joe said. "Only they have more people."

"We could have just as many, before very long," I said. "In about a minute, we could. Margaret Sanger's mother lived through eighteen pregnancies and eleven births, did you know that? Nobody cares whether poor people have birth control."

We were practitioners of birth control ourselves. I hated nothing more than having to buy feminine hygiene products like jellies and foaming tablets—I'd wait till a woman clerk was on duty in the drugstore and whisper the words. They were too graphic, those products, like artificial versions of private natural processes. I was sure it was wrong that such items should be made for profit and sold in stores for cash.

I was thinking about the capitalist system having this intimate contact with my own tissues, as I took the tube out of our suitcase and padded down the hall to the bathroom to slip the manufactured gel inside me. I tried to be fast, so Joe didn't wait too long, but a kind of modesty always kept me from doing this in his sight.

"It's ridiculous we have to do things with chemicals just to make love freely," I said to Joe, when I was getting back into bed. "It makes me hate nature."

"Don't tell nature you said that," Joe said.

"I hate it that procreation has *any*thing to do with sex," I said. "Who thought that up? What sense does that make?"

"Our opinions were not consulted," Joe said.

"There are too many babies," I said, "born every day and they don't get cared for and nobody does anything about it."

"I wouldn't say nobody," he said.

"You haven't been to India," I said. "You haven't seen all the babies in India."

I hadn't seen all the babies in India either, as Joe well knew. I did have a memory of a row of mothers and little children (littler than I was) sleeping along a narrow street, curled on blankets in a settled way, as if they were camping at a relative's. My father shuttled us past them very swiftly.

And why was I going on about this now? Dorothy had been so radiantly emphatic about how happy she was, and here I was having a fit about excess infants. I was in a house with a garden full of nasturtiums and green squash, the clean smell of salt all around, the frogs and crickets thrumming out the window, and I was mad at nature.

"Manhattan in August is every bit as hot as India," I said, a fact I made up, but I reached for Joe just then, so he didn't need to answer.

The next day we all took a walk along the beach with Forster. He pointed to a horseshoe crab, which looked like an iron helmet with a bayonet attached. "They're living fossils," he said. "Haven't changed for three hundred million years."

I thought the thing was dead, but Dorothy's brother John

poked it with a piece of driftwood and it moved very slightly
in the sand.

"Will it bite?" I said.

"Oh, no, never," Dorothy said.

"Its mouth is in the middle of its underside," Forster said,
"so it can't bite you unless you pick it up."

"It doesn't seem like an animal," Joe said. "More like a
moving ashtray."

"Forster said they can live to be thirty," John said. "But
they don't have babies till they're eleven."

"He knows a lot, that Forster," I said.

"I see hundreds of things on the shore much more clearly,"
Dorothy said, "because of Forster."

"He's the man to have by the sea, I can tell," I said.

Forster looked away. "He is," Dorothy said.

"Dorothy has extremely good eyes," Forster said. It was
the fondest thing I'd heard him say.

"How did you learn it all?" I said. "It's kind of amazing."

Forster shrugged.

"He went to shell college," Joe said. "They give you a wet
mackerel for a diploma. Leaves a lasting impression."

When we were back home again in New York, Joe would
sometimes imitate Forster picking up a crab or piece of kelp.
"It's very, very antique," he would say. "Its smell is older than
mankind."

Throughout that autumn I was aware of the months passing for Dorothy. I knew she believed that she was moving
into a larger truth, growing herself into a fuller vessel. And

the child would have the sweet, slightly neglected freedom the offspring of some of our friends had. If you did your best not to get in nature's way, would nature reward you? Our most theoretical friends liked to say the institution of the state was *unnatural*, as if no insult could be more utter.

Forster went out to Staten Island every weekend, even as the weather got colder. Betsy said Dorothy was looking wonderful. But Richard reported that Forster and Dorothy were having fights, because she'd started walking to town to go to Mass in the mornings. She mostly did this when he wasn't there, but he was horrified anyway.

"She isn't even a Catholic!" Betsy said. "If I were her, I'd maybe just not bother to tell him about this little secret church habit. I'd keep my mouth shut, if I were her. At a time like this. Where is her brain?"

"He'll never agree with her," Richard said. "Forster of all people. She knows that."

Dorothy had no cagey feminine practicality. She was more like a prophet, helpless to resist telling what she saw. My father, when he was a young man, had wanted to preach in India because (my mother told us) he couldn't bear not explaining what he knew. We all thought Dorothy was moving backward, and yet it was a poetic motion. "She's becoming medieval," Norman said.

Dorothy's religious eccentricity had an interesting effect on me, it pushed me into a different stubbornness. I stuck closer to my husband, very close indeed (where would I be without such a husband? how would I live?), and this meant going to more meetings. They had their bits of beauty, those meetings, especially the ones for Sacco and Vanzetti, where the rhetoric was already a wail of grief, though the two men, in prison, waiting, were certainly still alive.

In December Dorothy moved back to the city with Forster, and with her younger sister, Della. I liked Della, who was staunch like Dorothy but milder and girlier. It was Della who later went with Dorothy to Bellevue Hospital, when the labor pains came. Where was Forster? No one seemed to think he had planned to go anywhere near the yowl and blood of delivery. But everyone said he was entirely enchanted once the baby—a healthy girl—was actually born. Well, who didn't like babies?

When Joe and I visited Dorothy at her apartment, Della was holding the baby—a creature so tiny she could rest along Della's forearm—and walking her around the living room. Dorothy was lying on a couch and Forster hovered in a doorway. It was a small room, with all of us in it. "Who thought I'd have such a pretty baby?" Dorothy said. "I thought I'd have some gnarled little thing only I could love. You don't think she's too pretty, do you?"

"Definitely overdone," Joe said. "See if you can feed her something to make her homelier."

Della put her in my arms, as a great favor, but I was less eager to hold her than they thought. She was chubby and damp, sweet as my own baby brother had been, but I didn't want her curling too close to me. I knew perfectly well how babies were made, but I seemed to be afraid they were contagious. Joe said, "Look how she settles in."

"Hello, hello, hello, Tamar Teresa, hello, my fatso girlie girl," Della said.

I asked Forster how they'd decided on the names and he looked surprised. "Dorothy's work," he said.

Joe said, "How calm the baby is."

The baby took that as her cue to begin fussing, and Dorothy got up to take her out of my arms. "You little fat thing, you want more to eat," she said.

Dorothy swiveled and turned her back to us when she bared herself to nurse the child. Dorothy a mother! Forster led us into the kitchen and poured us shots of brandy. Joe said, "To the future that's just arrived," and we drank the stuff down.

Joe said, when we were out the door, "I think he really looks very happy."

"In his way," I said.

"He likes seeing Dorothy so glad."

"Richard thinks love is making a fool of him," I said.

We were all upset when we heard that Dorothy had made friends with a nun on Staten Island and had the baby baptized at a church there. Neighbors came to the beach house afterward for a celebratory lunch of boiled lobsters and salad, but Forster, who had caught the lobsters, left before people got there.

"He didn't have to rain on her parade," Betsy said. "What does it matter to him if she likes Jesus?"

"She's the one who won't stop talking about it," I said. "And it's his baby."

"He left on principle," Richard said. "I don't blame him."

• • •

Joe and I stood with a group in Union Square, trying to get people to sign petitions to the governor of Massachusetts, begging him to stop the executions of Sacco and Vanzetti. In a light summer rain Joe and I took turns holding an umbrella over us. Some people signed and were friendly. Some boys threw clods of mud at us, which we tried (to everyone's amusement) to block with the umbrella. Joe believed in acting jolly about it.

I looked at our flyer with its portraits of Sacco and Vanzetti, the two of them cuffed together, staring ahead, deep-eyed, men fond of gardening and known to nurse sick kittens, men neighbors said were too gentle to have shot two other workers for payroll money. Probably. Plenty of people I knew were sure the most dearly held principles had to yield to larger principles, that sacrifice was necessary for any radical change, even the sacrifice of mercy to violence.

I was against ever giving up mercy, and I thought the old kind of anarchism was done for. The point about Sacco and Vanzetti—anyway—was the government's unrelenting malice. I got wet and dreary and discouraged, standing out with our petitions. No wonder people like Forster never volunteered for this.

Really, as I saw it, Forster might just as well have stuck around to eat a lobster or two for the baptism lunch. Melted butter, hot rolls, crisp lettuce from the cottage garden. I thought he meant to stay for the meal but then he couldn't do it: he had no polite lying in him, not even for love.

• • •

Dorothy would have to be married in the Church, if she was really going to join the Church. No more cozy common-law in the beach shack. Betsy said Dorothy was painting herself into a corner, tying herself into an obedience she didn't even believe in. I barely knew any Catholics, not as close friends, and I didn't think Dorothy did either.

Sometimes I prayed when I was alone, a fact Joe didn't know. Not to any deity—I was done with kowtowing to whatever ran the universe—but sometimes I pled for help or for mercy. And in moments of great sweetness I would think, *Thank You for this*. After Joe and I were married, when we were alone, after the reception, in a hotel room with a ceiling of looping plaster garlands, I thought that.

We hadn't even meant to be married, had we? But then we'd made our concession, we'd given way on a point we decided didn't matter. It turned out we were that kind of people. Sometimes.

Forster kept leaving Dorothy and coming back. This went on for months and months. What did I want him to do? Terrible for a woman with an infant to have to put up with that. Didn't I want Dorothy to have him? But hard too for him to put up with Jesus all the time. Did I want him to find solace with me? Even in my dreams I couldn't bring myself to think of leaving Joe. In my fantasies I had a torrid affair with Forster, our dazzled bodies falling into one audacious discovery after another. But my mind got stuck on where we would go to act out these exquisite inventions: Didn't he still share the apartment with Della, when Dorothy wasn't there? Or had they all given that up? Could he be living alone, on his crummy earnings? I could foresee so easily every step in our falling into bed together, the hesitations and overtures and bursts of truth. But I puzzled over what bed we would use. The practicality of my nature worried the problem.

I had no special reason to think Forster was drawn to me. I had sometimes had glimmers, but I didn't think I was worldly enough to gauge them. The deepest question—which was not even a question but a blot over thought—was what it would mean to deceive a person like Joe. Even if he never knew.

But still I might do it. It might not be beyond me to do such a thing. Who knows until the tests are given? My mother used to say that India had tested her faith. The place was hot and terrifying but Jesus still lived. Once I told Joe that India had given me my own faith. I meant the leper. I was in a horse cart on the street with our maid when one came up to us, with his parched skin mottled light and dark, hobbling against a cane because one foot was missing. I knew about lepers from the Bible. His begging bowl was on a cord around his neck, but the maid had the cart go faster, to get away. At home I wanted my mother to find him and give him all our coins. My poor mother, I had a crying fit when she wouldn't. Joe said Emma Goldman told people she became an anarchist after she saw a peasant beaten with the knout, when she was a girl in Russia. Horror eats you, if you don't have an idea: that was what I thought.

·   ·   ·

Joe believed in using city libraries, and we were on our way to the Ottendorfer branch one Saturday when we ran into Forster on the street. It was October by this time and he looked all right—thin, but he was always thin—and he said, "This is the best season in New York, isn't it?" I thought it was a cheerful thing to say, and the sky was indeed a rare deep blue.

"It must be still beautiful out at the beach," Joe said.

"It would be, if we could be simple again, but we can't be," Forster said. "When I go out to fish, Dorothy has the nun come to visit her. The woman runs off if she happens to come when I'm there."

"The sister comes to teach Dorothy?" I said.

"Oh, yes, she does," he said. "Often."

"How's the baby?" Joe said. "She's all right?"

"Tamar is excellent," he said. "She's taught herself to crow at the gulls."

"The gulls probably know what she's saying," Joe said.

"I bet *you* can talk to the gulls," I said to Forster. "You of all people."

"Who'd want to?" Joe said. "Bunch of complainers, those gulls."

"At least they're not bowing and cooing to idols and statues," I said. "Gulls don't strike me as Roman Catholic types."

"What a thing to say," Joe said.

"You think I insulted the gulls by comparing them?" I said.

"Oh, Vera," Joe said. "Stop pandering."

It was very true I didn't sound like myself, I was helplessly overshooting to let Forster know I was on his side. And it wasn't the kind of tone Forster liked either.

"It's the pigeons that are more papish," I said. "Bobbing up and down like that."

"She still prays when she visits her family," Joe said, about me.

"Only at certain times," I said. What dolts Forster must have thought women were.

How exposed and absurd I felt afterward. Was I going to launch into flattering stupidities every time I saw Forster? Was I a helpless besotted creature? I had no respect for that sort of helplessness. It fit with none of what I believed or leaned on. Like not being deluded. Like the great question anarchists asked the world: Can't you do better than that?

I tried a new secret discipline with myself. For each time I thought of Forster, I set aside two cents to give to Joe, who was trying to save enough for us to get our own apartment. I thought Joe would be glad if I took more of an interest, and I could do without hoarding change for silk stockings. But there were too many illicit thoughts to keep track of, and it was too depressing to tally them when I did. So I underestimated and lumped the sums together in a dollar I gave to Joe at the end of the week. "What's this?" he said, surprised. "You don't have to." But he took it.

In August 1927 Sacco and Vanzetti were put to death in the electric chair, and the person who took this the hardest, of all of us, was Forster. He was out in Staten Island with Dorothy, and he went for days without speaking or taking food. He sat out on the bay in his fishing boat, in a stupor of despair. Some nights he slept on the beach. We heard this from Norman, who heard it from their neighbor. The neighbor said he did still like to play with the baby.

But how could it have been news to Forster, what human beings were? Where had he been all his life?

"If he'd grown up in India," I said, "nothing would surprise him."

Joe said, "He has a good heart but he needs to toughen up."

"He's not weak," I said. "Why do you think he's weak?"

"He should be infuriated instead," Joe said. "That's the whole point of what we go around telling people."

"Well, don't call him weak," I said. "That's all I'm saying."

"Is it?" Joe said. "You can stop saying it, then."

In November Dorothy and Forster had another serious fight about where her beliefs were taking her, and he walked out on her again. I could hardly believe he spent the night on the beach in the middle of November. When he came back, Dorothy wouldn't let him in the house. She locked the door against him. It was hard to imagine the two of them in such a drama. People who never shouted in ordinary life, reduced to harshness in a religious war. The next day she took the train into Manhattan and left the baby to be watched by her sister, and then she went out to the church in Staten Island and was baptized. She went through all of it alone, with only her friend the nun to be her godmother. We heard all this from Norman, who had a friend who was close with Della.

"I hope she's happy," Richard said, not nicely.

"I feel sorry for him," Norman said. "Outrivaled by Jesus."

"Bet she finds someone else," Richard said.

"How could she find someone better than Forster?" I said.

"She just did," Norman said.

"She has his *baby*," Betsy said. "It's very cruel."

"Oh, the man will land on his feet," Joe said.

And I saw Dorothy not long after, pushing a carriage in Washington Square. It was winter again, with the park bleak and windy, and the baby, already a toddler, was almost invisible under the wool blankets and knit cap. A soft pink face with closed eyes and a double chin. "She looks warm," I said.

"That's why we're here, it's too cold out by the beach," Dorothy said. "Forster used to chop all the wood for the stove but I can't manage all that."

"No. How could you?"

"Forster was a great wood-chopper. He'd hack up a big pile of driftwood for me to use all week."

"He must miss you and the baby," I said.

"How do you know?" she said. "Have you spoken to him?"

"No, but Richard has. I think he's fine."

"He's always fine, he's very healthy. Did he ask about me? Forget I asked that."

"Richard didn't say. Forster always keeps his cards close to his chest anyway. You know. Never one for loose talk."

"He thinks everyone else talks too much."

"Maybe we do."

The wind was blowing her hair from under her hat. "I think you love him yourself."

"What?" I said. "No, I don't. Not that way. I don't."

Everyone knows, I thought. There are fewer secrets in the world than people think.

"I probably don't really want to know," Dorothy said. "I'm just forcing you to lie. It's pointless of me."

"You have this wrong. Believe me."

"And then it will hurt our friendship," she said, "that you've lied to me. I'm making a mess, I'm sorry."

"No, no," I said.

"Never mind," Dorothy said. "It doesn't matter."

We stood there, in our awkwardness. How much she must want Jesus, I thought, to have let Forster go like that. Our Forster. I couldn't think of anything to say that wasn't more lies.

Beneath us Tamar made a little snorting noise—she had her face screwed up in distaste at finding herself awake. "Are you thinking of crying?" Dorothy said, bending down to her. "Think again."

"How big the baby's getting," I said. "She's so pretty."

"Bigger every day," Dorothy said. "I can hardly keep up."

That winter, I was much admired for my willingness to take the dog out to the park in any weather. Bakunin didn't care how many times we walked past the bench under the gingko trees to see if Forster was there. Dogs like repetition, it doesn't feel futile to them.

All through the holidays, when Joe and I went out to parties, I looked for Forster, but I only saw him once that season. On New Year's Eve, one of Betsy's friends held a masked ball in her apartment. Joe and I appeared as a dog and cat, with socks pinned on for ears. I saw Forster when we came in, leaning against the wall in a corner, but when I went to talk to him, he was already gone. When did he ever like parties? He'd only come before because of Dorothy.

The next day, Joe and I sat around the big apartment kitchen, trying to cure our hangovers with cups of black coffee, while the others slept.

"Everyone liked that party but Forster," Joe said. "Who comes to a costume party in street clothes?"

"Well, that's him."

"You just think he looks so dignified in his regular old jacket. That beat-up thing he wears," Joe said.

I did think that. Exactly that.

"The thing with Forster," I said, "is that he's sure he's too good for everything." Was Joe even listening? "I think he has to get over that."

"Do you?"

"He's too full of himself by half," I said. "You know what I mean. That expression of disdain he gets."

Joe was nodding. It was excruciating to see.

"But people like him change. He can get better," I said. "Eventually." I seemed to feel a note of condescension would help.

"You think so?"

"Absolutely."

"Right," Joe said, as if he believed me, as if he'd been reassured. Maybe he had been. For a second. He clearly wanted all this very badly—why else would he keep asking? He sipped his cooling coffee.

And what was I? What wouldn't I say? No one had held a knife to me and made me betray Forster, but I leaped to do it, to speak against him. No matter how dear he was in my heart. I placated my worthy husband with denunciations. I looked at the kitchen and thought that the scene of it would always be with me. The cupboard half open, with a canister of Swee-Touch-Nee tea inside, the oiled black gas stove with its red and white box of Diamond matches. Already I hated all of it, and I would see it again, tomorrow and the next day.

"Come walk outside," Joe said. "We need to walk." And he reached to hug me as I stood up. We leaned against each other like that, in a long, silent marital embrace, as if we understood one another very well. It was not a soothing moment for me.

I couldn't stop thinking of Forster, with his handsome squint, leaning against a wall in his old gray worsted jacket. Well, goodbye to that. Dorothy was in my mind too, as I'd last seen her, walking through the park, her wool scarf blowing in the wind, rising to the occasion of what she had wrought, rising to her renunciation. I'd done my own renouncing too, if a person wanted to think in those terms, but it was my own business, it was now and always my own.

Later on, when I had children, I used to tell them: Well, you've done your best, that's the main thing. I was repeating what I always said to myself. A person in favor of fairness has only certain routes. I didn't give myself any special credit for sticking by my husband, but quite a few of the marriages of our youth didn't last. The boldness of our thinking gave people too much faith in their impulses. Betsy made a very noisy exit from her life with Norman, and ran off with the man who owned our favorite speakeasy. He was older and not all that good-looking, one of the sillier passions someone like Betsy could have. We still saw her in the neighborhood, and she always referred to Norman as "the little genius of the masses," as if mocking him made her case. I thought she was shortsighted, but she did remain with her new husband, to everyone's surprise. Later they owned a hotel in Palm Beach that was supposed to be very famous.

Joe and I stayed anarchists, during years when not so many people were and others found communism more interesting. We tried to keep all our friendships, but there were hard times, during the Moscow trials, when we were very vocal against Stalin, and then during the Second World War, which we opposed. Richard, who was Jewish, would not talk to us for several years. In the war years, our two daughters had to face jeers and bullies who waited for them after school, and once a bag of dog excrement was thrown at one of them. It cut me very badly to know that. But we stood by what we'd always thought, when plenty of people didn't.

Norman, of all people, wrote a book about his lost youth in the best years of the Village. *Village Days and Nights*, he called it—not much of a title. In it he referred to me as "a shy young thing who blossomed under attention from any males of the species," and I told everyone I'd been called worse. Many pages were devoted to Dorothy, though I didn't remember that Norman was an especially close friend of hers. But when you know someone who becomes famous, those memories grow more details.

No one could have predicted that the person most visited by fame would be Dorothy. In the early days, she seemed to want just the reverse—she stopped showing up for picket lines, she stopped going out to drink with us. We were no longer very fascinating. But at the height of the Depression, when certain streets in New York looked more and more like India, she and a friend started printing up a newspaper called the *Catholic Worker*, dedicated to the untapped theory that the Church had more to say about the poor than it was saying. Their tabloid sold for a penny and was full of Dorothy's reflections and also little essays in free verse, about what Jesus *really* taught, by the oddball visionary who was her friend. (The two of them weren't lovers either.) The paper was a runaway success, and within a few years they had launched their next project, Houses of Hospitality, where the poor were fed homemade soup and the homeless were given beds at night, and anyone who walked through the door was greeted as Christ. People showed up to volunteer, and followers set up more and more of these houses, in cities throughout the country. Dorothy Day was a famous spokesperson, traveling all over, a propagandist for Works of Mercy.

But I didn't exactly believe in mercy. I thought it begged the question of why people had to be given what should have been theirs all along. I thought it tended the wounds of a violent system and helped keep it going, in years when such systems might've gone under and risen as far better things. I thought all the glory over giving away soup was myopic and misguided and ignored what really needed doing.

I did know, and even Joe said, there were worse things than people getting a few free meals—or being saved from freezing to death on park benches—while they waited for the revolution. Which (we knew by then) was going to be a very long wait. The great future was tarrying, like the next Messiah, and perhaps we were like Dorothy, in our patience. I had my old jealousy of Dorothy, but I revered (what a word) the way in which she had thrown herself into the fire of her ideas. She was burned down to Idea, all work and messy effort and silvery dedication. People thought she was saint-like, though being called that always made her say something scrappy and blunt.

And there was no man after Forster. She had probably expected another marriage—she liked men—but she became more and more a sister in her own order. We saw Forster on the street once, taking a pretty little girl of maybe eleven to a street fair, and I knew at once she was Tamar. I'd heard he took her for outings. She had fine, soft hair, clipped back from her forehead, and she looked skinny and quiet. I had my own girls with me, who were little then, dressed in nice sum-mer rompers. Forster said, "Vera! There you are," when he saw us. He didn't look all that different—lean, rumpled, with his high forehead and squinting eyes. "Long time no see," I said. We kept asking how each of us was—fine, fine—while the girls eyed each other.

"It's very hot today," he said to the girls. "You don't like ices, do you? Probably not."

They roared their protests to this notion, and he bought us all paper squeeze-cups of fruit ices, pale lemon and deep-red cherry, which Barbara, my youngest, got all over her. Louise, who was almost seven, dared Barbara to put her front teeth into the ices for the count of a hundred. "Don't," I said. "Do not."

"Did you ever do it?" Louise said.

Ices had not been a feature of my youth, but I confessed to sticking my tongue to a frozen iron banister in winter, on a dare from Mary Elizabeth next door. I didn't know why I had to tell them, except that I was always eager not to lie. We had once sent them to a kindergarten run by anarchists where they were told every day to be truthful.

Forster had taken a napkin and was busy trying to clean up Barbara's cherry-stained face, without much success. The sight of this was so sweet it unnerved me entirely, and I had to drag the girls away before I acted peculiar in front of everyone.

Later my girls entirely forgot that they had met Forster, though they'd liked him fine, but they always remembered the story of my licking a frozen banister on a dare. Another version of their mother! They teased me about it for years. Joe joined them. And I couldn't help liking being admired for any sort of courage, which it turned out we would all need, over and over.

The Hanging Fruit

So now we have the whole world going broke or already gone. Right in the twenty-first century, when people thought profit was so scientific. In a magazine I saw a page of cartoons on the financial meltdown, and one showed a bum on the sidewalk—same scruffy guy with a bottle in a bag who's always in cartoons—and next to him he has a sign: HAH HAH HAH. I tore out the cartoon and put it up on the door to my apartment. Neighbors kept stopping me in the hall to say, "Anthony, that's so great, I love that." Little did they know I used to be that bum. That is, I used to panhandle, when I was young. I did it in Paris, which made it seem less sordid, even to me. But the French can be stingy as a people, and their cops are every bit as mean as ours, so it had its bad days.

•   •   •

I was born in Palm Beach, by way of irony. My parents ran a hotel. They started it at the end of the Depression, when I was a baby, and it was a big deal in the late forties and early fifties when I was a teenager. It was a hulk of stucco built to look neo-classic—like a White House with palm trees—famous for its water views and its Nesselrode pie. The colonnaded lobby was packed with tanned, overdressed guests, all of them eager to call my mother Betsy, to rush at her on sight, to be tickled when she granted favors. Which she didn't always. She was a little queen of her domain, my mother.

I had two older sisters, Gigi and Ellen, and they both liked working the front desk, smiling away (sometimes they recognized an actress), but they were too earnest and silly to be as good at it as my mother. I was the one boy in the family, lazy and pensive and unathletic, and I hated the desk, I hated wearing a suit. When my mother was around, she would chat up the guests and then treat me to bits of cattiness about them. ("Is that a new haircut or a squirrel on her head?") But she loved their money, she loved the ring of their names, she loved their parades of suitcases. Her conversation was full of retold incidents and small quotes inflated. Her politics had once been leftist and she still had streaks of those views—she gave everybody a day off for May Day, she let people with Jewish names stay at the hotel, and she refused to let us buy gum because it was an empty commercial product. My father used to sneak us Juicy Fruit.

My father ran the bar and the restaurant. He loved hanging out all day and night, and he liked to think of passing the hotel on to me. Once he had me play my clarinet for Rita Hayworth, a favorite star of his, who was visiting the hotel. I wasn't a bad player. Happy birthday, dear Rita. On other nights he sat with me on the terrace, smoking his Havana cigar, praising the moon. I liked the moon well enough, but I was immune to the magic of the hotel. From the time I was little, I knew we were the servants of rich people.

I went away to college in Miami, not that far away but far enough. I lived in the dorm, with the rowdiness of other boys (I knew how to drink but I was quieter about it), and I loved the way Miami was a real city, each neighborhood its own planet. I was supposed to be studying business administration, but I was out walking the streets, eating Cuban sandwiches and conch fritters and pastrami (which I'd always thought was a joke, not a real food). The mess and noise of the outer world were a great discovery to me. I wanted to leave school right away, except that the first girl I dated told everyone that I used to party with the son of the Secretary of the Interior and I knew a lot of dirt about Cary Grant. These were exaggerations on her part, but other girls wanted to hear more. I'd say, "No, it's stupid," and they'd say, "Oh, come on," and next thing I knew I was telling some very attentive blonde about Rita Hayworth's drinking problem and what her daughter looked like.

Word went out that you had to know Anthony (me) very well before he would "confide" in you. I began to feel princely and wellborn. When I went home for Thanksgiving I was the least sullen I had been for years. I was dating three girls at once! Sophomore year I fell hard for Melanie, a lively person with a fabulous way of kissing, and in the course of sleeping together we became engaged.

It wasn't my worst idea either. Those were heady times for us—all the fun of sex was mixed in with our sense of being golden: we had luck and we deserved it. We felt a little sorry for the other kids, who hadn't found what they wanted and didn't even know what it was. We had already come into our own, our true and continuing inheritance. And she wasn't a stupid girl, my Melanie. She loved music and knew much more than I did—she introduced me to Miles Davis and Ahmad Jamal and Big Joe Turner. Like millions after us, we made love with those records playing, and then, when she sat near me in sociology class, she'd hum a bar into my ear, our private language. Unlike me, she had a very exact sense of pitch and could imitate any sound.

I still thought my classes were taught by nincompoops, and I never would have shown up for them if not for Melanie, who said, "Just get through it, get it over with."

"They're wasting my precious time," I said.

"Think of it as a savings plan that will pay off later," she said. We were both used to waiting. Being young then was waiting, it was the end of the fifties.

My mother liked Melanie's style—direct and sensible— but she had to tell me that the girl might be a gold digger. "I think you might have delusions," I said. She did, about Melanie, who was not a grasping type, and about the hotel, which, for all its booming success, was a mom-and-pop operation, not a corporate giant.

"Melanie could do a lot better if she wanted," I said.

Of course, I believed she could do no better than me. Who made her moan in bed, who could get her laughing at anything, who bought her a very excellent hi-fi for her birth-

day? And when I graduated (okay, I had a few credits missing, I wasn't in the ceremony), we could marry right away,
because I had a job and a place for us to live, a sunny, peach-
colored suite on the second floor of the hotel, in the back. I'd
paid just enough attention in my classes to decide we had to
modernize our billing and receiving—my mother balked but
then relented—and I went through the days quite pleased
with myself. All the guests, even the staid and desiccated
ones, liked to brag they'd known me since I was knee-high.
And now look at me, man of the world, cool as a cucumber,
married.

Melanie, who didn't have to keep house or cook because
we lived in a hotel, became my dad's ally in managing the restaurant and club. They had long conferences about whether
to change the house band and what music the square audi-
ences would tolerate. Melanie liked being useful, she wanted
a little importance, why not? My dad liked it.

We didn't take our honeymoon until the next spring, and
it was Melanie's idea to go to Paris for two weeks. "You think
I'm made of money?" I said. She pleaded (this was not like
her) as if she were my child: "Oh, pretty, pretty please, with
a cherry on top." And in our daze after our long, long plane
ride, how beautiful the city of Paris looked, old and stately,
dirt-streaked with history, full of nonchalant strangers parad-
ing for us. We took a nap in our hotel, woke up, and looked
out our balcony at the spangle of streetlamps and lit windows
in the dark. Melanie said, "Here we are, sweetie."

But no place is perfect, is it? A heavy, gusty rain poured
from the sky the next day, and by afternoon it struck us forc-
ibly that we really did not know much French. The rain kept

on, day after day. Prices were low, but people cheated us, which bothered me more than I wanted it to. In my head I kept tallying bills I'd overpaid, I couldn't stop. A saleswoman seemed to swear at Melanie when she was trying on gloves. Over and over we were stymied and confused, our confidence left us. We lost each other outside the Louvre. Melanie said, "I was *waiting*—can't you keep track of *anything* here?" when we found each other back at the hotel. These were ordinary mishaps, but we were not ready to be anything but victorious and clever, cherished by all. We left France with a vague feeling of shame.

Once we were home, it was very wonderful to me to have my old boldness back. I wisecracked with our busboys, I was charming to tittering dowagers, I drank till very late and made Melanie get up and look at the moon. "There's no better view in the world," I said. "Name one." I had us go out for drinks in other hotels, to feel myself recognized, to draw the greetings of management. When Melanie didn't come with me, women sought me out; they came up to my table to ask when we were getting a bigger pool or whether I liked the whiskey sours here.

That was how I took up with Debbie. She was only nineteen and first sat at my table with her mother, who wanted to know the best place to buy a panama hat for her husband. Debbie was a perky little blonde with a big bust, and I didn't know why she decided to fix on me, but she found me in the parking lot an hour later and made up pointless things to ask me. I was drunk but not dumb and knew not to risk making a pass, though she kept me there awhile. Of course, the whole encounter stayed in my brain and when she came to visit me at the hotel the next day, I snuck her into an unused room. What did I think I was doing? Taking more than I needed, piling on extra. People did. She was not even as pretty as Melanie, and nowhere near as smart. I lived in a sea of extra helpings, on an island of the overfed.

Debbie would lie on my chest and call me pet names. "Baby boy." "*Mon amour.*" "*Mi corazón.*" A year of junior college was enough for her, but she liked languages. Her family was booked for the season, so our affair had a whole winter to bloom. And she decided to be afraid she was breaking my heart. "Don't look so sad," she said. "I mean it. Give me a smile."

I liked my wife as much as ever. I never didn't like Melanie. The sight of her stepping out of her shoes at night excited me; I was even more attentive, more stirred up. "Wild man," Melanie said.

Did I feel guilty? I was too fascinated by what I was doing. I think I felt heroic, a man equal to a double task. I had passed beyond what was usual. Would I ever go back? I wasn't sure.

Debbie and I had a room in the hotel that was sort of our room, and I had the maids put flowers in it, hot pink gladioli, anthurium with curved red spikes, orchids with spread sepals and speckled labella. How sexy those flowers were, in an abstract way. Our affair had that kind of abstraction, it was intense and simple. We didn't need to know much.

The front desk had been told not to rent that room because the plumbing had an unfixable leak (much tee-heeing from Debbie about this excuse). "The number 716 is going to make you so lonesome after I leave," she said. She was going back to Wilmington, where she lived.

"We could meet in your town," I said. "I'll go."

"No promises," she said.

All the workers in the hotel knew about us, but no one was carrying tales. The night before Debbie left, I went back after supper to the chambers I shared with Melanie, and my wife was lying on the bed in her clothes. "Do I look green?" she said. "I feel green."

"What did you eat?"

"It's not the food," she said. She turned her face to the wall.

I had a very disturbing thought, but I let it go. I didn't say, *Are you pregnant?* I said, "Sleep, my lover." And I went off to see Debbie. She would be gone so soon, what did any of it matter? I had the rest of my life to minister tenderly to Melanie.

Debbie was giddy with triumph on her last night. "I'm going to make you remember me!" she said. This meant added flourishes in foreplay, which I certainly appreciated—much slyness and laughing, and then the more serious drama, the wild unstoppable resolve, the whimpering and calling out in voices not our own.

When we were done, Debbie whispered into my shoulder, "How will you ever get along without me?"

"Very badly," I said. It did occur to me that I had a lover to go home to and she didn't.

"It was not very bright of you to get married so young," she said. "Really very stupid."

"Stop it," I said. "Okay?"

"Why were you so stupid?"

"Debbie," I said. "I think it's time to shut up."

"You shut up," she said.

"I will, then," I said. "If you want."

I turned away, but not for long. There she was, when I turned back. Her tanned face was radiantly pink and misty with sweat.

"You just look so sad," she said. "I hate to see you look so sad."

I made a dopey sad-clown face. I was a little appalled at myself.

"Poor baby," she said.

I crumpled my brow, I turned down my lips in a pout. How greedy I had gotten.

"Cheer me up," I said.

Before dawn, I went back to Melanie, who slept in our bed, breathing evenly into her own dreams. Some hours later I came out of a deep slumber to hear her throwing up in the bathroom. "Honey, are you okay?" I said.

"Look at your back," she called out. "Just look."

I started to joke about how I didn't have eyes in the back of my head, did I, but by then I was swerving in the mirror and saw the row of scratches on my skin. Freshly rusty. I was sure there was a lie that would help me, but I couldn't think of it.

"You're the one I love," I said.

This only made her shriek and yowl—Melanie, the sanest of women.

She was still shouting, and her eyes were wet and furious when she came out of the bathroom. "How did I end up with you?" she said. "What's wrong with me that I picked you?"

"This was nothing," I said. "Really nothing."

"That's so reassuring," she said. "You betrayed me for nothing."

Melanie stood in her little flowery cotton nightgown, with her slender legs looking spindly, and I was more convinced by the minute that she was pregnant. I kept thinking, as she raged and twisted her face in disgust and I argued and cowered, that she would never leave me if she were having my baby. She was too solid a girl to maroon herself like that. I would do whatever penance I had to to keep her and she would never make it easy, but I would win her over in the end.

"Don't be upset, don't be. Tell me what you want me to do," I said. "I'll do anything."

"Give me all your money," she said. "Give me your salary for the rest of your life."

"Very funny," I said. "I guess we'll talk later."

"Talk is cheap," she said.

For most of the next week, Melanie had a stomach virus. She burned a low fever and threw up many times a day, and I came back to the room as often as I could to set down cups of tea, plates of dry toast, bowls of clear broth. Did she want ginger ale? A cold compress? If she was pregnant, she didn't say so. What she said was, "I'll be so glad to get out of this phony hotel and away from phony you and your phony family."

She got me to confess Debbie's name, and she didn't know who Debbie was. That seemed to especially enrage her. Her mouth was a bitter line when we talked. I held fast to the notion that she would come back to herself if enough time passed. My father paid a visit and brought her some favorite records to get well by. Tommy Dorsey, Miriam Makeba. She gave my father an earful about me. My father told my mother.

"Oh, Anthony," my mother said. "You were so nice when you were a little boy." I began taking most of my meals in our room. I ate what I could and I said anything I could think of to coax Melanie out of hating me. She lay slumped against the pillow, pale and fixed. I listed what was beautiful about her, I went into tales of great times in college, I gave her a soft, fuzzy bathrobe from the hotel gift shop. I bought her a very good pair of pearl earrings from the hotel jeweler. Even with my name and discount, I had to pay in installments, but the pearls were perfect and pure, her kind of thing.

The earrings were a big mistake. "Oh, no," she said, when she saw the box. When I finally got her to open it, she said, "You thought I'd melt with joy? You want me to crow with glee like a hooker?"

"You can exchange them for some you like better," I said.

"I'm not a hooker," she said. "You have everything all wrong."

And so I did, it seemed. Anything I said made things worse. My speed in getting into bed with someone else—after we'd been married *less than a year*, she kept saying—was an insult she could not get over. In truth, we were both at an age before we'd learned to get over anything. And I was undergoing the shock of knowing myself (me, Anthony) as the callous and unspeakable creep who kicked his sweet wife in the teeth.

Melanie, for Christ's sake. If I had dreamed for a second that she might find out . . . (another argument that didn't do much for me). I had never before been the villain of the piece and it made me feel abused by fate. I sputtered and fought, and when that didn't work, I glowered and spoke in sad monosyllables.

I did everything I could to keep her from leaving, but I could see she only grew surer that her honor lay in disdaining me. At night, in my exile on the couch in our suite, I remembered how glad she'd once been to see me walking toward her on campus, how her face would suddenly open and change into toothy joy. It was pretty devastating to remember. All my feeling for her was as clear and strong as ever, but now I was like a man in love with a movie star who didn't even know him. When she moved out with all her clothes and books and records and went back to her family, she said, "I don't feel sorry for you. But I will." She left behind her rings and an angora sweater with a fox collar that I'd bought her and the hi-fi I'd given her in college, which she said had always been crappy.

And I couldn't stand to hear any music now, it turned out. If I set down the needle, I'd take it up in a few seconds. Every tune sounded blithe and inane to me. But in the afternoon, when most guests were out, I'd go back to my room and put towels against the door to muffle the sound and I'd play my clarinet. I hadn't picked it up in a few years and my tone was terrible, breathy as a sick sheep. I kept playing the same simple tunes ("One for My Baby," "Autumn Leaves") until I was a little better. It was one of the few things I could stand to do.

And I gave Melanie almost as much alimony as she asked

for, despite the brevity of our marriage and the fact that she had left my bed and board. I did this out of sheer desolation. My lawyer was disgusted with me. Even my father, who'd always liked Melanie, thought I was a patsy. Maybe everyone did. The whole town knew my story. When I sat at our hotel bar trying to pace my shots of Seagram's so I didn't get too blotto with guests around, people tried to be nice ("Sorry about your troubles") and they commiserated about money. Men did. They'd say, "They soak you, don't they?" or "Freedom has its price, oh, boy." Women said, "You're young. Time for a new start, when you're ready."

It was fortunate I could drink for free at the hotel, since my cash had to stretch much further now. The weekday bartenders, an ancient and discreet crew, became people whose faces I knew as well as my own. Women did hover around me at the bar—I'd become someone to be curious about, to ask personal questions, to offer comfort or more than comfort, and it made me feel somewhat elegant, to be a man who turned down luxuries.

The thing was not to drink too much. I could get too confident, could hold forth about how Rita Hayworth liked me or how divorce is a racket for lawyers. I'd tell any woman in the bar she was a member of the smartest sex by far, that men were just dopes compared to females. One woman told stories about how they measured the intelligence of dogs (were men as smart as dogs?) and the conversation got so jokey and riotous that I ended up going back to her room and having an entirely enjoyable fling. She was gone within a few days, back to her husband, but a friend of hers knew about me and liked to joke with me, as if we had a secret. Pretty soon (the

steps were not that many) we began to have our own secret.
She too was married—her name was Kitty, a breezy, languid
sort of woman—and we had to be careful because the husband was sometimes about. She was not afraid of him but
I was. "He's a bluffer," she said. "That's what bankers are."
How spoiled I was, letting her tickle me under the covers.
This was an odd time for me—my heart was clotted with
pain, aching for Melanie, and I was somehow also having an
almost genuine form of fun.

The house rule, explicitly stated to all hotel employees,
male and female, was no fooling around with guests. Well,
of course not. Think of the trouble, the lawsuits, the tawdri-
ness. I understood the need to be careful. But one night I fell
asleep and woke up to the stench of burning fibers—I was
sleeping in a nest of flames! Kitty's bed was on fire, from one
of my cigarettes. I tried to keep myself from shouting at the
mattress while I hit it with a blanket. Kitty had the sense to
get wet towels, which worked better. By then the room was
full of black smoke and we had to run out to the hallway. I
was just getting my pants on when the other rooms emptied
out. People blinked at me in their pajamas. The firemen coming up the stairs cursed me for being in the way just as I was
getting the hell out of there.

I was back in my own room, safe and asleep, when my
parents woke me sometime early in the morning. "This can't
go on," my mother said. "You can't live here and keep this up."

"He knows that," my father said. They had let themselves
in and were standing by my bed.

"What did we work for?" my mother said. "What is this
hotel, then?"

"Nobody says you're not a bright boy, Anthony," my father said.

"They might do this in France," my mother said, "but not here."

"You got to get out of here for a while," my father said. "Go stay with your sister Gigi in Tampa. She'd love to have you. Dry out. You listening?"

My father used to run a speakeasy, and my mother was once the belle of Village radicals, to hear her tell it, before she left a husband and went off to mess around with my father. I wondered, not for the first time, where they had buried those parts of them. I was very, very thirsty and my head weighed four hundred pounds. "Is Kitty okay?" I said. The skin on my palm was oozing where I'd apparently burned it. My mother brought me a tumbler of water to drink. "Okay, okay, I'll go," I said.

I was in a secret rage at the hotel. It had been my ruin, that palace of quiet piggery. I knew this was a stupid form of blame, but every monogrammed towel, every sculpted brass faucet, every strain of piped music in the lobby now gave me the willies. Things I'd been around since birth seemed to me full of corruption. My parents were right: I had to leave.

But I certainly wasn't going to Gigi's in Tampa. Tampa and I didn't seem like a good match. I began to think Paris was the right idea. My mother and Henry Miller had put this particular bee in my bonnet. City of *liberté* and *chacun à son goût*. I was fairly sure I would like it better without Melanie.

• • •

I had no money for a ticket, unless, of course, I skipped this month's alimony. If a man happened to be behind on such a thing, was it illegal for him to leave the country? I had the feeling it was wiser to keep my plans to myself. The thing was to go soon and stay as long as I could. Not that I had any savings for such a move. But I was the one whose job it was to pick up the cash from the front desk, tally the accounts, and put all those greenbacks in the safe. When not all of it reached the safe, the ledgers (kept by me) didn't show any such loss. I had some guilt about doing this, some edginess as I walked down the halls with a secret lump in my briefcase. I did it five times, and each time the thefts also made me a little high.

I packed my clarinet in its black leather case, with a decent supply of reeds, and two valises. I told my family I was going off to Gigi's, and I drove to the airport and boarded a plane to Paris. Simple as that. My plane left at sunset, when the sky was hot orange and strange. What dream did I think I was in? I was drinking, or I might have treated my parents better, but what liquor made me see was not entirely wrong. The mess I'd made of things was from a spirit in me that could get grim and fiendish or could spill into a brighter night.

The unsimple part was that I had no idea at all what to do when I landed. I got lost in the airport trying to read signs with my high school French. All I could think of was to take a cab to the hotel where Melanie and I had stayed, that elegant hulk near Avenue Foch. How jaded I felt, walking again into the gilt-and-curlicued lobby. They had no room and sent me around the corner to a dowdier place, a curtained fortress of iron balconies. Tired as I was, I put pillows against the door of my room and I took out my clarinet and began to play "Au Claire de la Lune" very, very slowly. The skin on my palm was still stiff from the burn I'd gotten in the fire, but the slowed tune had a sweet drag to it. I waited for someone to knock and tell me to be quiet (I was afraid of French people being fierce), and no one did. And then I fell asleep in my clothes.

Early the next day, I woke up dull-headed but dazzled that I wasn't in Tampa with Gigi. I had to go out to the American Express office to telegraph my parents, to keep them from worrying I was dead. *HAVE TAKEN DETOUR TO PARIS*, I wrote in my telegram. Perhaps they would all be envying me my adventure.

I walked all day, following my nose, fueled on caffeine and a panic close to joy. How cheap things were here. I bought a pack of Gitanes for almost nothing, I bought a pitcher of wine at lunch for spare change. I settled on a bench in a park and watched a child and her mother feed pigeons. I must've looked very American (no European had a haircut that short in 1962) but no one bothered me, no one cared.

It was October, but I ate outside that night at a pretty restaurant with tables on the sidewalk. Some very good-looking women walked past me, while I savored my *entrecôte* and drank my Pomerol. One went by in a chartreuse coat, and I said, "What a nice color." I said it in English, and she answered me by asking if I knew her friend Barbara in New York. (She said *Bar-bar-a*, sounding each syllable.)

"Oh, yes," I said. "I know her well. A lovely person."

"Maybe she says you are very nice too," the woman said.

She looked to be about my age. She was a pale girl with

blots of pink in her cheeks and dark hair neatly trimmed. There was nothing vulgar in her looks, and yet she was flirting with a stranger.

"I am a student," she said. "You are a student?"

I was not eating in a students' restaurant, that was for sure. I considered saying I was in school, if she wanted that. "I own a few hotels," I said. "What are you studying?"

She was reading American literature and she very much liked Hemingway and Faulkner (which she said *Foke-ner*). "You know where is Mississippi?" she said.

I said I was from Florida, which was farther south and even warmer than Mississippi.

"I like the warm countries," she said.

"Would you like to sit down?" I said. "Maybe have a bite to eat?"

This expression made her laugh—"Bite you?"—but she did sit. When would her studies be done, and what would she do then? "I will starve," she said.

She might have been starving now, from the way she ate the steak she ordered. She cut and chewed with charming speed. Did I enjoy Paris, she asked, did I want to see more of Paris, she could show me.

No wonder this city wasn't so great with Melanie, I thought. The woman's name was Liliane, and I wanted her to see my hotel, which I thought she'd admire, but the staff might give me a hard time if I took her to my room. Some hotels were like that and some weren't.

In the end, after we'd gone through more wine, I walked her (with my hand at her chartreuse back) to a taxi stand, and I gave the driver some bills to take her wherever she lived. She was coming the next day to show me very fine things. I got in some extensive kissing before she took off. I wasn't sure she was really coming back the next day, but I was okay with that.

The sight of her in my lobby in the morning was like a jolt of pure adrenaline, like a drug anybody would pay bags of gold for. She walked me all over the Eighth Arrondissement and the Seventh. I didn't really care all that much about churches—why did she think I wanted to see them?—but these were necessary foils to our actual mission. A chill wind blew leaves at our feet. She shivered with cold in her char-treuse topper, and I showed off by gazing into the window of some illustrious store on the Rue de Rivoli and buying her a very snappy red wool coat right then and there. I admired the casual way she slipped on different models, her lack of cloying thanks. Once the coat was bought, we were more intimately tied.

I wouldn't have done this at home—buy an expensive present for a woman I'd only just met. At home I didn't have to. Everyone knew who I was. Here I was unknown even to myself, at the perilous start of who could say what. Her English made my English more stilted, and I had only my dollars to help me. I had to do what I could to make everything go well.

And so it did. We had a bang-up dinner in a bistro she picked on Saint-Germain-des-Prés and then she took me to hear jazz in a club, which was just what I wanted to do. I had to drink many coffees to stay awake, which sobered me slightly, and I heard, truly, the saxophone waiting, talking, waiting, while the drum muttered back and the bass laughed at them. I'd heard better groups, but not in person, and my skin could take in all the vibrations, my breath followed all the bypaths. Liliane said they were having a good night.

It was perfectly natural to go home to Liliane's. She lived in an ill-lit and probably crummy neighborhood (where were we?) in the tiniest apartment I'd ever seen, a closet with one window and a hot plate. "Welcome, Mr. America," Liliane said. The bed was soft, a pale grove of softness, and I passed out before we did very much.

I was in better shape in the morning. As a lover, Liliane was playful and poised—well, I might have guessed that. Was she freer than American women? Maybe a little. She was, I would say, less serious, less stagy, and less afraid to walk around without her clothes. "You are happy?" she said to me, as we sat up in bed, sharing a bottle of water. It was not an intelligent question, but I didn't mind it, I didn't mind anything.

"Sure," I said.

It was not a lie, not at all, but a few other things I said were. I told her my family had a hotel in Algiers and one in Vienna. I told her I'd gone to Yale, which she'd never heard of. Why did I think my freedom was in making things up? I enjoyed my own stories. Liliane probably didn't believe everything either. The fire that burned the hotel in Palm Beach to the ground, the crazy wife of mine who pitched a diamond necklace into the Atlantic Ocean—"*Mon dieu!*" Liliane said, but not convincingly.

And was she really in school? Sort of. She said she was

reading for exams without going to classes anymore. This gave her plenty of time to lie in bed listening to the radio after we made love, and she was free all that week to drink aperitifs in the lobby of my hotel or in cafés where she knew people. Her friends were perky waifs of women (they bubbled at me in what English they had) and two or three males who looked a little too amused by me.

It was a few days before I remembered to check at American Express for any word from my parents. Indeed there was a telegram waiting with my name on it. *ASHAMED AND DISAPPOINTED. LETTER TO FOLLOW. MOM DAD.*

I had not expected such a violent response and this suggested—strongly—that they had discovered the thefts, which I really had not thought they would do. A wave of horrified surprise came over me, as I walked outside clutching my piece of yellow paper. What made me think I could fool anyone ever? What wool did I think I'd pulled over the eyes of my parents, of all people? Then a Frenchman whose way I was blocking said something brusque to me and I said, *"Je m'excuse,"* not nicely, and the sound of my own voice made me remember: *Well, I'm here and they're there.*

Liliane was waiting when I got home, and in bed I was a little more reckless that day. I moved in a trance of interesting suggestions, which she fell right into, laughing and expressing what I hoped was gasping admiration. The room was dark by the time we were done. Out the window I could see a strip of purple dusk. Liliane said, "My crazy boy. Wake up. Don't sleep now." She got up and made us what I called cowboy coffee, boiled in a saucepan and poured through a strainer. It made a streaky mess in her chipped sink but it smelled delicious. It was the first time she had done anything domestic.

It reminded me I wasn't going home to America anytime soon. I wasn't about to live with Liliane—it was too hard to imagine ever truly getting to know her—but I might settle in one of those hotels people stayed in for years. Some place homey and reasonable, where nobody minded if I had guests. Maybe Liliane knew of such a place?

"Ooof," Liliane said, making faces at her own coffee. "Too burnt. Yes, many, many places. Only you to tell me when you are ready."

That night we went out late to meet her friends, and she reintroduced me as the new Parisian, fresh citizen of the world's greatest city.

"How long you stay?" someone asked.

"Forever," I said. "I'm going to cash in my ticket." I thought of this just then.

They all applauded. "A beautiful thing," Liliane said. I had not expected that—a table of people clapping for me. They told me I'd get good money for the ticket on the black market, better than any refund. One of the women knew a guy who would help. They toasted—squat tumblers of wine held before their faces. Paris forever. Sometimes, I thought, things fall into place very easily.

And Liliane took me to a hotel I liked right away, or pretty much liked, a place in Montparnasse that had very good rates by the month. The room had yellowing wallpaper and a sorry-looking bidet in the corner, but I was charmed (I could be charmed) by the old dark wooden bed and a beautiful little writing desk, and the window opened to what felt like a secret courtyard. Liliane helped me move—we stacked my two valises in a taxi, along with a huge rubber plant I'd bought in a moment of alcoholic enthusiasm. One of the valises was actually full of cash, since I'd brought over my funds in the most literal, bulky way. I carried my clarinet on my lap. "You are Mr. Benny Goodman?" Liliane said.

"I'm much hipper," I said. And when we got to the hotel, after we ascended in that rickety cage of an elevator, I sat on the bed and played "Till There Was You" for her on the clarinet. I tried to sound like Jimmy Giuffre. It was a simple, tenderly plaintive tune and some feeling in it survived my amateurish playing.

"Is that for me?" she said. "I thank you for that."

I was suddenly thankful to Liliane herself. Without her, where would I be? In her offhand way, she had helped me into a different life.

We drank shots of some very decent cognac, sharing the room's one water glass. We took a nap, and woke as the light from the window was fading. A motorcycle seemed to be revving up in the courtyard right outside. Liliane said, "When I first come to Paris, I thought was so noisy. But now I don't hear noise." I'd always thought she was from Paris. And where did she come from? From a small town in Normandy with farms around it. "Very ugly town," she said. I saw she must have been smart, to get herself to a Paris university, though I didn't think of her as smart.

"Was it too boring there?" I said.

"I don't like there," she said.

"You won't go back?"

"Oh, of course," she said. "To see my family. I go sometimes."

I remembered my own family then, whom I thought about surprisingly little. I was still waiting for the letter-to-follow, but then I hadn't checked the American Express office since the telegram, had I? I sort of hoped they were forgetting me too. Other people could do my job—Millie in the office, or Luís, the front desk manager—my parents were nothing if not practical. What if I never went home? I would tell them where I was, I would always do that. This resolve made me feel better, insofar as I needed to feel anything.

I went to American Express the next day to send home the address at the hotel. *My current digs,* I said in the telegram. *Write me here.* And there was a letter, yes, held for me under my name. I saw the envelope with the hotel's logo of a red palm tree. *Oh, Anthony,* my mother had written. They had fired Luís, a very dignified guy with many children and grandchildren, for stealing from the intake. That was before they discovered the truth. Imagine having to tell everyone what kind of son they had. *What were you thinking?* my mother wrote. *Forget I asked. I don't want to know. Right now I don't want to know you. Love, Mom.*

I hadn't been thinking, not in the ordinary sense of that term. I had seen a way to proceed, through a few brief steps, and none of them had been what you'd call difficult. At the time it surprised me that I hadn't done such a thing before. So easy. Luís had taught me to ride a bike, he'd worked at the hotel for years. *No one told me they would blame you,* I wanted to say. I couldn't keep from saying it on and on in my head.

That night I told Liliane that Palm Beach was a town of beautiful houses and handsome beaches, but my family did not treat its workers very well. I'd quarreled with them over this, and that was why I left. "You are not like them, then," she said.

"I guess not," I said. "My sisters are more like them than I am."

"You are more generous," she said.

"Well, anyone is," I said.

"They don't have unions in America?"

"We have them."

"Here we have big strikes," she said. "Some people don't like them but I like them."

"You just like people making trouble," I said.

"No, no," she said. "I am for unions."

"A strike isn't a party," I said.

She gave me an insulted look. It made her mouth tight and her eyes oddly bright.

"France is not afraid of strikes," she said. "Better than America, I think."

"Why don't you just go give your new coat to the workers if that's how you feel?" I said.

"I think you are drinking too much," she said.

I actually wanted to smack her. I'd never known I was a person who could want such a thing. Was this what I'd come all this way to learn? That notion was so depressing I couldn't move, except to close my eyes.

"I go home and you sleep," she said. "You can have a good sleep now."

"You're very clever," I said. "Aren't you?"

She was already up from the bed, where we had been sitting side by side against the wall. "*Fais des beaux rêves,*" she said. "*Pas de cauchemars.*" She was wishing me to sleep. And she found her too-good coat and got herself out the door.

·I wasn't proud of myself the next day. Liliane had no phone at her place—you had to leave a message with a friend down the street, not an English-speaking friend—so I'd have to go in person later to apologize. I knew perfectly well that I was drinking too much. If I started later in the day, I could cut back significantly. And use my days better. Since I wasn't going home anytime soon and my money (though it was holding out nicely thus far) couldn't last forever, it might be time to learn more French: Take a class? Find a tutor? And eventually I could get a job in management in one of Paris's many, many hotels. One of the big regal places or a small adorable one. I'd be around different people then—Liliane's friends were really quite limited—and I would settle into the city more deeply, more thoroughly.

It was cold when I finally ventured out, a blustery November afternoon with the light fading quickly. Liliane's building, a four-story slice of soot-dusted stone, was at the end of a narrow street, near Boulevard Voltaire. From the hallway I heard voices, and when Liliane opened the door—"Allo, it's you!"—

I saw she had Jean-Pierre and Yvette with her, a couple I'd met maybe once before.

They were laughing about something that had happened to another friend. His wife had left him, which did not sound that hilarious to me. Oh, if I knew, they said, it was very funny. But they were speaking in French, and I was lost. Liliane had me sit in her one dining chair—the room was crowded with all of us in it—and then sat on my lap. I was glad and relieved to see her so friendly, so sunny.

And she was very lively all that night. We went to a restaurant that had oysters—much joking about their aphrodisiac effect ("I will cripple this man if I eat another dozen") and much bragging about how she used to gather oysters as a girl and carry baskets home. Jean-Pierre said, "Always a strong girl," and Liliane wanted to lift the table to show us, but we stopped her. Yvette was choking with laughter and had to be given water.

We were out very late, and when I was back in my hotel room with Liliane, I passed out in my clothes. I was dimly aware of her taking off my shoes and pants and I was touched that she was tending me. When I woke up the next day, she was gone—it was already noon and sunlight was pouring in from the courtyard. The room was underheated and I had no reason to get out from under the covers. I stayed in, eating crackers and chocolate and reading a detective novel (Mickey Spillane) and snoozing off and on until the next day.

I was up at daybreak, and the windy walk to the café on the corner for coffee convinced me that I, the famous coat-buyer, needed a new one. The Florida version of a topcoat wasn't going to cut it here, and this gave me something to do that day. I unlocked the valise with my money in it—I was thinking camel's-hair would be nice—and when I lifted the lid, the suitcase was empty. The piles of bills, bound with rubber bands, were not where they had been. I thought for a minute I had the wrong suitcase, but I didn't. Had I gone and moved the money, in some drunken theory about a more secret hiding place? I forgot a lot of things I did. It was possible I'd put it under the mattress. Or I could've wrapped the greenbacks in plastic and hidden them in the high toilet tank. The labor of lifting the mattress—not there—and climbing above the toilet—not there either—made me sweat in the cold room. I was yelling, "Shit, shit, shit!" over and over. The cash wasn't in the drawer of the writing desk or on any of the shelves of the big chiffonier. It wasn't under the bathroom rug (well, I wouldn't put it there). I was shouting all the time, and I groaned as if I were ill. I *was* ill, buzzing with the heat of mounting anguish.

There were two maids, a handsome old one named Mireille and a plain young one who would never tell me her name. It wasn't the maids. Probably not, I really didn't think so. If I asked Liliane, would she say it was the maids? I drank what was left of a bottle of marc and I went downstairs and bought a token at the desk to call Liliane from the pay phone off the lobby. Liliane's friend said, *"Pas ici!* No more!" That was as much as she had ever actually spoken to me and I couldn't get her to say anything else. *"Pas ici!"* Not here.

Okay. I had to go find Liliane in person. I could threaten her, I could push her against the wall. *Listen to me.* I could call the American Embassy! They would laugh, wouldn't they, at another poor horny bastard duped by one of the local girls. *Oh, Liliane*, I thought. Had she hated me all along? Was it hate-sex we'd had? If so, I hadn't known. She had been an eager and athletic lover but not coarse or strange. And I saw how naïve it was to think she had robbed me out of hate. No, the money had tempted her, the money had been too beautiful to resist. The golden abundance, the hanging fruit.

Had she ever seen me go into that valise? Had I left it open in front of her? I didn't know, how could I remember such a thing? I was lucky I remembered where my shoes were in the morning. Or she might have snooped while I slept, which was not very pleasant to imagine. That lock could be pried with a bobby pin. It was too much money for someone like Liliane to ignore. Once she knew it was there, the fact of it must have burned in her mind all the time. All the time.

I got on the Métro to go to Liliane's apartment. The subway was filled with women in angora mufflers and shining boots, men with combed hair slicked back with tonic. I was the unshaven, sullen one.

At Liliane's building, I rang the bell over and over, and I banged on the door and yelled her name up to her window. Nobody on the street was happy about this. An old man in a woolen cap scolded me in hisses. I wrote a note on the back of an old restaurant receipt and wedged it into her mailbox. *Call me now—urgent—Anthony.*

Back at the hotel I sat up in bed, drinking and smoking and counting how much money I had in my wallet. Enough for five days, maybe longer, depending on what I ate and drank. My room was paid up for another two weeks. There were things I could sell. I had several books that could go to the English bookstore. The rubber plant had been bought at a street market and might be set out on the sidewalk again. I could make a sign that said for sale. EN VENTE. I knew that much French.

I hadn't eaten for some time, and I went to the nearest grocery store to stock up on what could be downed cheaply in my room. Hard cheese, dry salami, a tin of sardines. Red wine of a kind I had not stooped to try before. When I was back in the room, chewing my foodstuffs at the writing desk, I felt less crazy and weak. I began to think more about Liliane. She used to kiss my toes, laughing! We were not done yet. If I could get her attention, I could shame her into giving the money back. She might, after all, hide it again in the room and pretend it had only been lost. Once she saw me again, once she remembered what there was to remember.

I went back to her building later that night and rang the doorbell for ten minutes. I showed up the next morning, and my message was still stuck in her mailbox. I showed up that evening too, as if it were my work in life, but this time I walked all the way, which took an hour, including my getting lost. I wore a heavy sweater under my light wool topcoat and buttoned the collar as high as it went and kept my bare, frozen hands in my pockets. I rang and yelled her name, I rang and yelled. *Liliane. Liliane. Liliane.*

I was glad to come back to a bottle of wine in my room. Alcohol kept me warm and stopped most of the fear; it brought with it a spreading certainty that fear was beside the point. Not that I was deluded. I still knew what a mess I was in, but I also knew how to slip into this other understanding of the facts. I respected the wine for that.

I could scale back. I was a well-nourished person and it was not going to hurt me to live on less for a while. A fresh baguette was better than cake. Let them eat cake! I could offer Liliane a lovely wedge of crusty bread if she came back.

I didn't have an airline ticket home anymore, did I? Her friends had probably cheated me on that too. But Liliane must have believed I had only to write home for more. (And what would I say? *Dear beloved family, You'll never guess what—that money I robbed from you has been stolen! Believe it or not.*) And I knew if I had the ticket again, I'd turn it in for a refund. I wasn't going home. That part was over.

I scared the maid when she came in. It was the young maid, a lumpy person with drooping cheeks, and it startled her to see me with a crewneck sweater over my pajamas, lying on the covers with a clarinet next to me. "Hello there," I said, a little sloppily. She said something I didn't under-stand—nothing friendly—and took to her heels. No clean towels for me.

I played "Since I Fell For You" on my clarinet and my tone was not bad. I played it over and over. The hotel manager came to knock on the door. "*Silence, s'il vous plaît.*" He used both languages. I didn't answer him, but I tried just fingering the notes and not blowing through the mouthpiece. Later in the day I tried stuffing a handkerchief in the bell of the clarinet to muffle it. Didn't work.

· · ·

In the long evening hours, how hard it was to lie there and not play. At twilight I went out and took my clarinet in its case. A few blocks from the hotel there was a small triangular plaza with a few bare trees, and I sat on a bench and played "The Pajama Game." My fingers got stiff right away and the cold was bad for the instrument, but I could play any way I wanted. Soft, loud, it was my own business. A woman smiled as she went by. A man about my age stopped in his tracks to listen. He stood with his hands in his pockets, nodding. Then he put fifty centimes in my clarinet case! This struck me so funny I choked on the chorus.

I bought a package of nuts with the money and I went back to my room, tickled at the story of this. In my head I was telling it to someone, but who? Maybe when I was feeling more alert I'd write to Melanie. *Hey, Mel, you wouldn't believe what's been happening.* Not that she'd be looking for anything in the envelope but a check.

They wouldn't let me stay at the hotel any longer. I wasn't even sure my full month was up, but the manager said, "Tomorrow we say goodbye, you give the key, happy journey." *Bon voyage* to him too. How slimy he was. Was it possible for me to extend my stay, perhaps in a different room? The manager really did not think so. *Non, non.* The hotel was very full, many guests. Busy season. A line I had used myself.

They didn't want my money, and I didn't even have any money. I got a minor chuckle out of this. When daylight began to fade, I went out with my clarinet to the windy street and then down into the glorious warmth of the Métro station. People were packed in at that hour, no room to sit, so I leaned against the wall, tired as I was, and began "Baby, Won't You Please Come Home." The clarinet resonated beautifully in that underground chamber—it startled even me—I held the long notes. *I have tried in vain/Nevermore to call your name.* What a great song. It took a while before one high school kid parted with a coin, and then I became a trend, the guy you had to appreciate. I took one break to buy a pack of peanuts from a vending machine, which perked me up nicely, though the salt wasn't great for playing. I stayed in that station for a couple of hours, filling it with music.

On the way home I smelled the buttery enticement of somebody cooking crepes on the street, and I bought a plain one. It was the best thing I'd ever eaten in my life, steaming and softly chewy and perfect. I'd had a good night, hadn't I?

So I was in an upbeat frame of mind when I got up the next morning. I asked the snotty desk clerk to please watch my luggage until I came back for it, and I hit the street, wearing my layers of clothing and toting underwear and socks mashed into the clarinet case and a small bottle of brandy in my pocket. I knew that I cut a ridiculous figure but I felt secretly competent at this job I had invented for myself. I played the clarinet very well for someone who played in the subway. More than adequately.

Before I was halfway down the stairs to the station, I could hear an accordion player below, blasting his chords into everyone's eardrums. I decided it was my day to work the trains, and I hopped on the first one that rolled in. Riders were not pleased when they saw me take out my clarinet, but I played a few bars of "Have Yourself a Merry Little Christmas" as if I were alone in a room, my eyes straight ahead. When I was done, I walked up and down in a matter-of-fact and professional way, with the case held out for cash, no smiles or imploring.

Then I got off at who-knew-what stop and started again on another line. In the afternoon I started to play "Eine kleine Nachtmusik." Poor Mozart. What would Mr. Jefferson, my old clarinet teacher, think if he could see me here? But it was a crowd pleaser (French people clapped!) and I used it again all day.

In the Métro stations, I could stay warm, use the underground pissoir, have my slugs of brandy in private, and get packaged candy from the vending machines. I could even smoke and very few people minded. There was a lot to be said for the Métro.

But the trains didn't run all night. There was the flaw. I pretended I didn't know they were shutting down and I curled up to sleep on a bench. It was not really that uncomfortable, and I felt slightly superior to all the people who were so sure they needed things. I knew better and I was stronger. People really had no idea.

I was asleep when a voice started shouting at me. I jerked awake, but I had already made the shouter impatient and he hauled me up and slammed my spine on the bench. The pain shocked me, it buzzed into me with an electric cruelty. By then I saw he was a cop, in his navy uniform with the pants tucked into those heavy boots, and my body went sick with fear. He was snakelike and thin-necked, with a sharp, expressionless face. He was pushing me to go somewhere and he kicked at my ankles, but not as hard as he might have. I grabbed my clarinet case and started to run toward the stairs, and that seemed to be what he wanted.

I was terrified enough to keep running in the street, banged up as I was and limping like an idiot. I wasn't made for this, I was the wrong person for it. In the wintry air I was wildly thankful that I had at least remembered to grab the clarinet. I was out in the cold now.

On the street, the stores were gated with metal bars, the upper stories dark. In the distance I saw the shapes of two young men walking, with their hands in their pockets, turning to each other and talking loudly, laughing at something. How had I stopped being one of those men?

I was trapped inside a mistake. When was it going to end? *Liliane, Liliane, Liliane.* I was shouting in my head, not out loud, but I gazed up at the glass windows of buildings: she might be here as well as anywhere. Where was she? Or Melanie could come get me. Maybe I could get in touch with Melanie.

But I had money on me, actual francs—how had I forgotten this? If I could find a café open at this hour, I could drink and be all right. I had only to walk and I would find one. This did not turn out to be true, but moving around was warmer than staying still. I stopped at a massive stone church, a hulk of spires and leaded windows, but the door was locked fast.

No room at the inn. I was outraged, not that we'd been much
of a churchgoing family. My mother dragged us every so often
to an Episcopal congregation but we never paid much attention. I sat down on the steps and leaned against the building.
The stone smelled musty in an interesting way in the cold.

When I woke up, the darkness had just begun to turn
blue. A few steps below me was a shape rolled up in a blanket, which I knew must be another man. He was too close—
I could hear the rise and fall of his breath, there was menace
in the sound. And where had he gotten a blanket? Were they
giving out blankets? He was too tightly rolled for me to try
to steal it.

He stirred in his covers (I didn't like that motion) and
his head emerged, the dark eyes widening at the alarming
sight of me. *"Bonjour,"* I said to him and raised my hand in
a wave. The man muttered something—it wasn't *bonjour*—
and closed his eyes. He wanted me out of his sight.

When I woke again, the sky had the pinkish tinge of
dawn. The blanketed figure was still on the steps below me.
I was sober enough now to be properly scared of whoever this
was. Under that cover, he might well have a knife or a razor.

Was he moving? The dirty wool of the blanket was
stamped HÔTEL DUBOIS, where he must've once slept. When
he sat up, I saw that he was younger than I was, lank-haired
and scrawny and gaunt, with a nasty scrape on his cheek.
He glowered at me, and then he seemed to chuckle at how I
looked. The chuckle was what chilled me. I stumbled to my
feet and got out of there as fast as I could.

Later I thought that I might have offered him a cigarette—
I still had a pack with me. In every movie, people did that. Or

I might've dug the half-eaten chocolate bar out of my pocket and given it to him. He would've taken it. As it was, I fed myself a loaf of bread I bought on the corner, but I could've come back with it. I didn't do any of those things, and it was a long time before I became someone who did.

I tried a new strategy in my music that day. Underground, high notes rang clear and low tones got lost, so I started out with Benny Goodman hits, lots of upper-register toodling. Playing fast (which I did pretty sloppily) impressed those Parisians. People thought I was working for my money.

At night, I walked till I found a very small, grim café, and I feasted on a plate of strong-smelling, gristly sausage, the cheapest thing on the menu. The café had its clientele of rugged, methodically hard-drinking men who looked me over but said nothing. When the owner was urging everyone out, I got him (with some body English) to sell me a bottle for the road. I was already sleepy from having eaten so much, and I knew the wine could be my blanket when I went out into the street. I was providing for myself as well as I knew how.

Some of the men in the café had wolfish faces, and I worried about being helpless in sleep. I clung to the notion that even the outside of a church might be safe, and I didn't have to walk far till I found one. I settled across the step under the carved archway. *This can't go on, I can't do this anymore,* I thought, as if there were someone to plead with.

I woke up puking. I had to get upright fast to keep from

choking, to keep from drowning in the sea of my own fluids and half-digested sausage. I leaned forward as far as I could to keep from fouling my coat or my clarinet case. All the expense of the meal, spilled out and wasted. My convulsing guts had no mercy, what I might have called my self was taken over by a rage of systemic revolt, and I was not done for a while.

If I had money, I thought, I wouldn't be a bag of sick and I would be asleep in my bed. I knew I was a drunk, but my family's hotel had been full of drunks, whom we'd helped up the elevators to their cushioned chambers. They probably slept very well. I was nowhere near sleeping, and I was shivering. I thought of going down to the river and dipping my hands in the free waters of the Seine, to splash my face and get myself cleaned up.

When I got closer to the river, I saw the problem. The night hadn't broken into morning yet, and when I looked down from the sidewalk, the riverbank below was entirely dark. Trees rustled, something else rustled. I wasn't going into that span of blackness, not me.

So I kept walking. I was a coughing creature, carrying his clarinet case by its dinky handle. Holding his coat tight, a laughable piece of prey. *Get me out of here,* I thought, and I meant out of my own useless, shivering body. I'd had enough. And I didn't want Melanie to see me like this. I knew she was in Florida, I wasn't deluded, but when two girls in high heels clattered by, I lowered my head in case one of them was Melanie. Probably streetwalkers, and they didn't want to see me either. They went into one of the world's grungiest hotels, a four-story shack of peeling stucco, with a lurid orange neon sign, HÔTEL DUBOIS. The what? A hotel short one blanket, stolen by my friend in the street. Recognizing the name amused me so richly that I sat on the railing of the quai to contemplate it.

If I could clean the puke odor off me, if I could get a little more money, it was a place that would take me. It did not look very picky. I must've believed the street had already swallowed me, that I'd never get back into the ranks of those who slept indoors. I had to see a flophouse to remember I might aspire to it. I couldn't see anything that wasn't in front of my face.

When the sun rose, I went to the Gare Montparnasse, and I used as much soap as I could in the men's room, despite the stares of other patrons. I worked a long time over my coat with a wet paper towel. Then I went out and began my musical patrol of the subway cars.

I stopped before the evening rush hour started. Nobody wants to give money on a crowded train. I bought mints so they wouldn't think I was a drunk and I made my way to the Hôtel Dubois, which was not that easy to find again. But there it was, looming out suddenly, ashen white in the dimming light, its sign unlit and wiry. If they didn't want to take me, I'd figure out how to ask if they knew another place.

The clerk was an old woman who said almost nothing, and only wanted to know if the room was for me alone. No one else? She wrote a price on a piece of paper. I handed over the francs for one night, and she gave me a key and pointed toward the stairs. I could go up, just like that? I couldn't quite take it in.

The stairway was dark, past the first floor, and I had to fish for the light on each landing and walk fast before it went out. The room they'd given me was bare as a stable, except for a metal-framed bed, a table against the wall, and a sink in the corner. Mine, my room. I fell on the bed at once—how irresistible it was, the mattress and the creaking bedsprings, the scratchy blanket, fitting itself against my back. I thought about what a *room* was, and the essential brilliance of the idea astounded me. Wall, ceiling, floor. I couldn't get over it. I was not getting up for a while.

In the morning I stopped being just a creature, which involved soaking my head in the sink to get it clean. There was a shower in the hall but you had to pay to use it. The toilet, also in the hall, was a porcelain hole in the floor, and I met some of my fellow guests waiting for it. A Swedish guy with a beard like a beatnik's and a frowsy Belgian, bare-chested in his pajamas. Weren't there ladies? The Swede (who had good English) said the hookers used the first floor. I told my name, Anthony, and it surprised me to hear the syllables. He was still around, Anthony?

Back in my room I had my wake-up swallows of alcohol, and I thought, as the glow went down, that I was going to have to watch out now. No passing out in these halls. On the other hand, I couldn't be sober or I'd never get myself back out on the subway trains. I still looked ridiculous, with my layers of sweaters and my stretched topcoat. Later I'd go back to my former hotel and retrieve my goods.

• • •

How sweetly familiar my two valises looked to me, when the snotty clerk dragged them out from a back room. "You have also a message," he said. From Liliane? I was grinning like a fool, and I realized I had put my hand over my heart. She wanted to explain, she wanted me back. Maybe she hadn't even taken the money, it was someone else. Not her fault.

Hello, Anthony, you don't know me, the note said. It was not from Liliane. *Your mother suggested I get in touch with you. I used to be married to her, long ago! Now I live in the 6th arrondissement. If you get this, come by to visit.* It was signed Norman Remsen, with a phone number.

I knew full well who he was. The first husband, from her Bohemian youth. My mother always said he'd been wise to leave town before writing his memoir that offended everyone, certainly including her. So now he'd been enlisted to offer me a touch of home?

I wasn't grateful. In my days and nights on the street, I took one step at a time and I could keep track of those steps. I had become stupid and literal and I liked it. I wasn't ready to give it up.

Of course, the note made me think about my mother. In her "Village days," as she always called them, my mother had lived in a big mess of an apartment with a bunch of other young paupers. "You wouldn't believe the cockeyed food we ate," she said. "Anything cheap." Insofar as she mentioned the husband, she suggested he was an empty blowhard too precious to earn a dime.

And here was this man who'd had sex with my mother and been told I was a thief and wanted to see me. I remembered to be glad that my mother was worrying about me. I kept that thought.

Meanwhile, back at the Hôtel Dubois, I went out every day (I was a very steady beggar, no time off on weekends), and the hookers would see me at the café next door when I came in at night. *Allo, cutie boy baby.* They didn't have much English and I could not have looked like a big spender to them, though one of them did offer a very low rate, in numbers I understood. She was still pretty, with tender skin, but her features had gone slack, loosened from their moorings. She spooked me: look at what she'd lost, to johns like she wanted me to be. The Swedish guy, whose name was Nils, said that Marx said prostitution was only a particular expression of the usual fate of the worker. She'd sold away something, anyone could see this, and who had it now, where was it?

Nils did help me buy a jacket at the flea market. He led me into block after block of awning-covered stalls selling sections of iron pipe, old petticoats, army helmets from who knew when—everything shed, left behind, spun off from the fat, fat world—and, at last, used coats. They smelled of dust and worse, but there was a navy wool peacoat that was only slightly too big for me. In the long mirror at the stall I saw myself, bony, red-faced, but better.

Once I had proper clothing, I seemed to feel I had to see

this Norman person, who answered his phone in French. "I hope you're having a very good stay," he said. Oh, I was, I said, and he invited me for supper later in the week.

I was drunk when I showed up. How else could I have gone there? I mounted the winding stairs to his apartment on Rue Claude Bernard, dizzy on the turns. I smiled in my blurry way to see Norman, a bald guy with glasses, and the nice-looking Frenchwoman who turned out to be his wife, an aging gamine with wispy hair in a ponytail. "You're here at last," Norman said. I was an hour late.

The rooms were small and cluttered with bric-a-brac. They had a piano and a seashell collection and one of those Indian elephant-headed statues in green china. *No wonder my mother moved on*, I thought. "Just a light supper," Norman said. "Nothing fancy."

There was nothing to eat! Some slices of salami for our appetizer, a cream of broccoli soup, a bunch of watercress for salad. Where was the rest? And Norman, it turned out, talked a lot. "I hope you've noticed how great the vegetables are here. You have, right? Of course, we take them for granted. But we didn't during the war. No, siree."

I almost said, *What war?* "You were here all through it? With all the Germans?" I said.

"Not here!" he said. "Not in Paris! It wasn't a good place to be a known anarcho-syndicalist."

A what?

"We went to the south," he said. "Josette has family in the south."

"Very nice to stay with them," Josette said. "More nice to come home."

Josette was a kindergarten teacher, so she had gotten work again right away. But Norman, who said he "wrote for some English newspapers," had had more trouble. But now was better. Now? The war had been over for seventeen years.

"A person misses Paris," Norman said. "So how long are you staying?"

"Forever," I said.

"So what do you do all day?" Norman said.

"The sightseeing gets old, but I've met a lot of great people," I said.

Josette said, "When you're young, you're free, you can see everything."

On the way back from taking a pee in their itty-bitty bathroom, I passed the big elephant-god statue on a table. It had a few coins lying around it—a fifty-centime piece and two francs—and I thought about plucking them out, but I didn't.

"One of my friends," I said, as I sat back down, "has a chateau on the Loire and I'm going up there for New Year's. Big grand ball in the castle. Should I bring a gift, do you think?"

Norman, who was carrying in a bowl of fruit, looked at me hard. "Great pears this year," he said. "Your mother always liked fruit."

"At the hotel we have this gigantic orange tree that grows right up through the lobby. And we imported nightingales to sing in it." I made this up.

Josette was setting out little plates with dainty knives and forks. Maybe we were getting a cheese too? We weren't.

"Your mother would think we were sorry fools, the way we live," Norman said.

"Oh, no!" I said.

"Your mother thought the world was made of winners and losers. We didn't agree on that."

Pretty clear what side she thought Norman was on.

"I hate the way Americans use the word *loser* now," Norman said. "They mean someone who's doomed because he won't push or grab or steal."

Josette, in her niceness, went to the kitchen and brought out a bottle of brandy to go with the pears.

"Let's drink to the superiority of losers," Norman said. So we did.

After a while, it was natural for me to get drowsy in my chair. Josette, with her accent, was talking about Algeria and the Left and I hoped no one would notice if I shut my eyes. I woke up at one spot and said, "No! France is not free, it's expensive!" I was making a joke. Josette might even have laughed.

I woke up when they were lifting me to my feet and leading me into the back seat of a very small car, which turned out to be theirs. Next thing I knew we were in front of the Hôtel Dubois, with its orange neon sign, though I didn't remember saying where I lived. I forgot how to get out of the car and they had to unpeel me and I hung between them going through the door. "Good night, dear hearts and gentle people!" I said as I headed toward the stairway. Past the first landing, I kept stumbling on the steps that went on forever and I was annoyed they'd left before helping me to my room, wherever it was.

· · ·

The next day I thought, *Oh, shit, another burned bridge. Dear Betsy, Your son is a worthless turd.* I got myself together to go for coffee at the café next door but I didn't even have enough money for that. Why hadn't I swiped those coins near the statue?

I saw then that I was going to keep getting worse. Already I was someone I wouldn't want to sit next to. The number of activities beneath me was getting less and less.

The next day turned out to be Christmas, and I slept through most of it (stupid, on a day so profitable for panhandlers), and at nightfall I showed up at Norman's with my clarinet. When he opened the door, I played an excellent, jazzy version of "God Rest Ye Merry Gentlemen."

Josette applauded. Norman said, "Look who's here, risen from the dead."

"I'm not dead!" I said.

They shepherded me in, and it turned out there was a whole table full of visitors—maybe their Lefty friends, maybe Josette's relatives, I didn't know. What a really, really bone-headed blundering jerk I was. But Norman sat me down and gave me chunks of lamb and potato and carrot, and everyone was speaking French anyway. Josette kept patting my arm and trying to feed me more. I was in one of those dreams where everything goes on in pantomime and nothing makes sense.

After all the plates were cleared, they pushed away the

table, and Josette sat at the piano. She was beckoning me to play with her! She took the tempi too fast, and my clarinet sounded better on "White Christmas" than on "Silent Night," but we were fine. Much smiling and applauding.

I thought I should leave before I drank more and before people tried any harder to talk to me. Thank you, *merci, joyeux Noël, merci, merci.* I was almost out when one of the guests decided he was going too.

He was a man Norman's age, but with more hair, a white crop of it, which he was tucking under a wool cap. And did he speak a word of English? I hoped not. We descended the stairs in silence. "You are the boy whose mother is once the wife of Norman?" he said.

Ah, the group had been entertained with tales of me. Hilarious. "Are you from Josette's family?" I said.

No, no. He was a very dear friend of Josette because they went to Hindu meditation together. Did I know what it was, meditation? No, Norman didn't go with them. Norman was against religion.

"Meditation is not religion!" he said. "Norman is old. Old head."

"I think he's very youthful," I said.

I really did not live very far from Norman and Josette, and the next week I came home in the evening to find them waiting in the café to take me out. "You're not a big spender, I see," Norman said, by way of comment on my hotel.

"I wanted to live differently," I said. This made me sound bold and adventurous instead of duped. I didn't tell them about

Liliane. Daily I held my hat out for coins on the subway and
thought I was beyond embarrassment, but apparently I wasn't.
Nor did Norman get to hear any accounts of my musical career
on the Métro. If I didn't have my secrets, what did I have?

Still, when Josette managed to drag me to her Hindu hoote-
nanny, which had chanting as well as breathing, I saw perfectly well what a relief getting free of my posturing self could
be and I was impressed by the kind of humble nakedness
they were chanting for. I imagined (for a second) rising out
of my own murk. But closing my eyes made me sleepy (I'd
known it wasn't a place I could walk into sober), and I started
talking during some sort of sermon in French. *I hate sitting
on the floor*, I said. *I could sit on the floor at home if I wanted.*

Poor Josette. Afterward a guy of maybe forty walked up to
us and said, "How you doing?" in American English. Another
American! "Oh, yeah," he said. "Lots of us in Paris."

"So I've heard."

He'd met tons at the English-speakers' AA meetings at
the American Church. Maybe I'd like to come with him
sometime?

I laughed. "Thank you, no." Not me, buddy.

Josette didn't laugh.

On the way out we passed another of those elephant-headed
statues, with the same fat belly and fancy headdress. I knew
the coins around the base were offerings, people betting
on their luck. All the meditators were pushing to get out of

there, and a twenty-franc bill was glowing, glowing by the god's dainty humanoid foot. It was worth maybe four dollars, and I couldn't imagine why someone had given so much. I palmed the money and kept moving. I looked sideways to see if Josette's eye had caught me. Her face was creased in what looked like anguish, so she'd probably seen. A nauseous heat spread in my chest, but I kept walking.

I walked home in the cold rain and I thought, *Money is killing me*. I knew it did no good to blame dumb objects, but the crinkle of legal tender in my coat pocket felt like a snakeskin, like a specimen swabbed with infection.

And back in my stall of a room, I looked at the bill, which had a portrait of Claude Debussy on it. One more dead musician. Should I burn the twenty francs? I had a box of tiny wax matches, and I lit one, just to think about holding the bill to it.

Who was I kidding? I lit a cigarette instead. Norman would say that property was the God of the bourgeoisie (I'd heard him say it) and that I'd grown up in a false church. This made me think of the hotel in Palm Beach, with its soaring lobby and its majestic brass elevators, its strutting guests calling out to one another across the veined marble floor, its doormen with military epaulets. I didn't imagine going back. Fucking everything up had changed me. I no longer believed in all that.

I wondered how Norman, that rumpled old renegade, had managed to be in love with my mother. Norman's ideas seemed basically right to me, as my mother must've once thought, though they'd failed to overturn anything in the world for very long. But Norman would never use the word *fail*.

Josette must've been very young when they met, a bright-eyed revolutionary dove. The thought of Josette made me groan. She loved her meditation group, she loved that elephant-god, blesser of beginnings and overcomer of obstacles. Why would I pay myself a lousy four bucks to wound Josette so badly? Josette, who had never been anything but kind to me.

The next day I woke up, hung over as a piece of road kill, and I used some of the twenty-franc bill to buy a bottle to clear my head. I had my work to do, didn't I? In the station, I had regulars who knew me, who nodded at tunes they liked. I was playing "The Pajama Game," very jaunty and coy, when I saw a woman who looked like Liliane. I was always seeing these women, but this one had a red coat exactly like the one I'd bought her. It *was* Liliane, with her dark hair grown longer, wearing bright lipstick and a pink wool scarf. She looked like a million bucks. She was good at that. I was horrified to have her see me this way, a rat-faced bum with his hat at his feet for coins, but I kept playing. Tootling away. She knew perfectly well who I was.

She moved till she was hidden behind a pillar. Very cool, but skulking. Not enviable, I thought. I could feel her there, the high-heeled shape of her, waiting. Was she afraid I was going to shout at her? Growl in rage about her crimes? In fact, what I'd always imagined, if we ever met again, was my saying something wry and flip. *Looking good, Liliane*. I didn't say it.

How relieved I was to watch her get on the train. *Please disappear.* The backwardness of this—that I was the one ashamed before the lover who'd robbed me—hit me very hard. In her seat on the train, I knew that Liliane was shuddering to herself, to think we had ever been in bed together.

My clarinet sounded like the wheezebag it was, and I had to stop playing. Enough music. And she'd tell her friends about sighting me—bring back the details for Yvette and Jean-Pierre. How long did I mean to keep doing this? How many times was Liliane going to be there watching? And that was the story I told for years, after I figured out which Métro line would lead me to where the American Church was, so I could just take a quick look at the schedule and see when the meetings were.

I stayed in Paris a long while after I was sober. I had the luck not to have many friends to begin with, so I didn't have drinking buddies to avoid. After my French got a little better, I got the side jobs that foreigners get. I waited tables in a burger joint full of noisy Brits and Americans, I tutored anxious French people in English.

I moved out of the Dubois, with the girls looking up from their drinks at the café to say, "Goodbye, happy trails, cookie boy." Before I left, I paid Nils back all the bits I'd borrowed. Much to his surprise.

In meetings I talked quite a lot about Liliane. I knew whatever she'd done was her own business, but I had to hope she had a regret or two. I had the idea that I was something Liliane had put in hock, that her awkwardness in the Métro had been like someone passing the pawnshop window with dear ticketed goods right out in front, hideously familiar.

Meetings were full of people who'd pawned their trumpets, their wedding rings. Their false teeth! Their children's cribs! What did you trade, what was your price? I myself had run out on alimony payments, a crime I hardly thought about. I wrote a letter of apology to Melanie, which she didn't answer. I wrote to my parents. I paid Josette what I took from the statue. I did those things.

I got promoted to manager at the burger joint, and I was so overqualified that someone hired me to run a *pension* that catered to international students. I liked that job. The girl students found me interesting, and I had more than a few romances, which nobody fired you for in those days. Then I fell in love with J.J., a fast-talking girl from New York who was studying anthropology, and she convinced me to move back to the States with her.

When I left France, Norman said, "May the next chapter overflow with freedom," which I later found out was the last line of his infamous memoir. In New York it was a shock to have English all around me, as if I'd been in disguise in France and now was exposed again. My secret ambition was to run a jazz club, and I began with a job taking tickets in a very decent one. I heard great players—my whole life unrolled in that music—but it was a bad place for a nondrinker. I fell off the wagon the first month. J.J., who was too young for this kind of crap, left in outrage that I'd turned out so different, angry that I'd tricked her.

I didn't feel very tricky. What was I in New York for, without her? Straightening up didn't bring her back either, no matter how many meetings I went to. But I saw I could stay if I wanted. My next two girlfriends were women I met at meetings. One of them found me a job in a coffee shop in a chain motel near the airport. I wrote to Josette, *I wear a white paper chapeau with great style.*

In my bad years, I ran a flophouse, a den of sadness, but I took some pride in running it well. I had more patience with the weirdos than anyone was used to. Most of the guys weren't bad guys, only a few were real trouble. I made the place homey, with a TV to watch in the lobby. My mother used to give me management advice over the phone. "It pays to be personable," she said.

At first my parents kept urging me to come back to Palm Beach. They gave up when it became clear to them that I was committed (as they put it) to looking constantly at unpleasantness. It was true I had lost whatever taste for luxury I'd had. Living on the street had done that to me, which is the reverse of what people think will happen.

I found my best job after I was fifty. I got hired to run a halfway house in Queens for guys coming out of prison, nonviolent offenders catching some fresh air before parole. It was a low-paying job—nobody cared that I hadn't exactly finished college—in a rabbit-hutch of a home owned by an agency. I liked to tell everybody I was in another branch of the hospitality business, and in fact the job was a very good use to make of me. Not everyone wants to keep house for a bunch of beaten-down fuckups, but I liked it. On Christmas I played them carols on the clarinet.

When my mother died, not too long after my father, I took a large chunk of the money they left me and tried to start a foundation to help the newly paroled. Maybe I got grandiose. Part of me did it to concur with Norman, that fulminating old fart, who always reminded me in his letters that he'd never believed in prisons. What was I thinking? I had years of experience begging, borrowing, and stealing, but I'd never overseen a budget, and, as it happened, I was a financial dodo. I couldn't seem to see my way clear about how to reserve funds for this and pay out for that—and my poor would-be foundation went broke before very long at all.

My sisters were more prudent and invested their share smartly, so that when they sent me photos in their emails, I could see Ellen's son had added a spa and exercise center to the hotel and Gigi, old as she was, was driving around in a top-of-the-line Mercedes. Her hair was a quasi-humorous strawberry blond. *Let them have this last surge of spending*, I thought, *since it makes them feel free*. I had nothing against their feeling free, I of all people. They'd taken to sending me books for Christmas like *The Total Money Makeover* and *A Guide to Prosperity*. They pitied my really quite happy retirement to a small apartment in Sunnyside, Queens.

I was as horrified as anyone when I heard the news on the radio, before I heard it from them, about how everybody in Palm Beach, including them, was snookered by this investment guy with a Ponzi scheme. How irresistible they all must have been to him, thrilled at his promises, delighted to know him (my sisters always used his first name), happy to feel his coins fall into their eager hands. What he really, really knew was how very much they wanted what he pretended to get them.

Who doesn't want money? I'd stopped wanting tons of it but I wasn't beyond wishing. I could have been one of his clients, me too, one more moron, easy as that. My sisters were not comforted to hear this. Oh, Anthony. Their whole lives, they'd never thought they were fools and now they were, in front of everyone. "Plucked like chickens," Ellen said. How did one guy make sixty billion dollars disappear? Gigi said, "It's a nightmare. I don't understand. Do you?" and I said (but they weren't ready to hear), "It's all right, it's all right."

Two Opinions

When my father was in prison, my mother took us to visit him. I was nine when he first went in, and my sister was six. Some of my mother's friends thought taking us there was a mistake. "The girls have to know," my mother said. "They're not too young. And why would I do that to Joe?"

My father was in Danbury, Connecticut, which my mother said was nicer than a lot of places, and he was there on principle. I knew what principle was. He was against the war, despite his despising Hitler and Hirohito as much as anyone ever could; he was against all wars waged by governments. He was against governments. He was an anarchist. Other people my parents knew went into the army as medics or did service at special camps, but not my dad, who wouldn't register for the draft before the war even started. I had a fair idea what registration was, but my sister didn't get it.

My mother dressed us nicely for these two-hour bus trips, in pleated skirts and Mary Janes, as if we were going all the way from Manhattan to visit a relative, which we were. We had never, of course, thought of our father this way, and Barbara, my sister, shrieked when she first saw him in those brown clothes that weren't his, with his mouth a tight line in his face. "Get her shushed," the guard said. "Or get her out of here. I'll say it once."

My father had an expression I'd never seen before, a wince of mortification. I made a zipping motion over my sister's lips, sealing them. "Hey, muffins," he said to us. We were in a visitors' room with a bunch of wooden chairs and several other families in dramas of their own. Our mother made us tell him what we'd done in school—Barbara had learned the state capitals, and I had come in second in a spelling bee, after Maxie Pfeiffer, who thought she was the top of the world. "Second is good," my father said.

We couldn't bring crayons or pencils or toys into this room, so when my mother wanted adult talk, she had me take my sister into a corner and tell stories to entertain her. "You can do it, Louise," she said. We sat on the pitted linoleum and I made up a story about a blue elf that made no sense. Barbara pretended to like it.

"Behave yourselves, kitten-heads," my father said when we left.

On the bus going home, my mother opened a bag with special treats—celery stuffed with cream cheese, ham sandwiches with relish, homemade brownies *and* date-nut squares, and a thermos of lemonade. We were very excited, the whole trip seemed to have been so we could have this food.

We learned to expect treats on every trip, donated by friends or baked by our hardworking mother at night. My dad was allowed an hour of us a month, which could be broken up into two half-hour visits. The visits had creepy aspects—our mother had to go behind a curtain to be searched; one of the prisoners had a face like a panther; the guards blocked us and made us go home the time we were four minutes late. All the same, we mostly looked forward to going. Our father was quieter there than at home—no rowdy games, no tickling—but he could tease us about our big feet or tell us we were more beautiful than Lana Turner; his voice was still his voice.

The kids in school were the problem. My father didn't care if the enemy bombed and burned and shot everyone in his own country. He didn't care who died among all the brothers and fathers who were fighting for all of us. I heard this all day every day from kids I didn't know and kids I did. "He's my *father*," I said. Maxie Pfeiffer dared another girl to punch me in the stomach. I had been taught not to hit, and my hands trying to shield myself just made everybody laugh. A teacher broke us up and sent the girl into detention (Maxie went free), but I was never safe at school. Barbara didn't have it easy either. Once they threw a bag of dog shit at her back.

My friend Ruthie's family wouldn't let me come to their apartment anymore. Ruthie said, "Does your father *want* Hitler to kill us? We're Jewish, you know."

"*I* know," I said. "I've only known you since you were five."

Her parents wouldn't let her in my house either, but we were old enough to go to the park in Washington Square ourselves, where we continued a game about cowgirls and runaway horses that we'd played for years. There was a grassy spot across from the fountain that we especially liked, and we met in all weather, out on the range in earmuffs.

None of this got easier as time went on. My father was sentenced to a year, and when he came home, my sister kept sitting on his lap every time he sat down, and I was always tap-dancing for him. I pursued him nonstop with the shuffle-off-to-Buffalo. There was a big party to celebrate his return, with music on the Victrola and my mother giggling. She kept working at the job she had now, sketching ads for a department store in Brooklyn, and our dad was mostly home, where he read a lot. I didn't understand what happened next. The law still wanted him to register for the draft—hadn't he already told them? He had to tell them again. He was home for six months and then he was back in prison.

My sister Barbara was a mess, so I had to be not a mess. I ignored her stupid whining and I acted very upright and prissy, which was a good idea—after a while she tried to imitate me and stopped being such a pill. My mother started to visit the prison more often without us. And in my dad's second year there, he was part of a work strike because he didn't like it that colored men had to sit separate in the dining room (my father told the *guards* he wouldn't work), and this went on for months, and none of us could get in to see him.

•   •   •

I was a teenager and the war was over by the time they let my father out. He had been a talkative man before he'd gone in; he came out shadowy and subdued, a phantom father. But then, week by week, he grew more distinct and animated, he spoke to us more often and more loudly. Sometimes he was newly bossy, checking to see if we'd made our beds, making us wait to eat till our mother sat down. We were a little afraid of him now.

In the meantime, I was starting to think about boys. In high school people still knew my father had helped the enemy, but some boys decided it wasn't my fault. I liked almost any boy who liked me; I couldn't get over the thrill of their interest, though I had been raised to be a serious person.

Various boys joked around with me after school or leaned over me on the subway ride home, but nothing came of it until there was an argument among the staff of the school newspaper, about whether we needed another article about prom etiquette, and this boy and I were on the same side (against it). He was a broody guy, with a nicely developed sense of irony, which allured me greatly. Walking on the street after the newspaper meeting (our side had lost), we did our own spoof of a student boob presenting a corsage and stabbing the girl with its pin. I clutched my chest and leaned against a stoplight, to act out my wound. He pretended to half carry me across the street, and all that horsing around was extremely interesting.

What was his name? Ted Pfeiffer. He was Maxie Pfeiffer's older brother! This twist of fate was not as jarring as the other known fact that came with it: the father in that family had been killed in the last year of the war. "I know your sister," I said.

"She's a complete pain," he said.

It wasn't until our third time at the movies, when he made a move to start necking and I absolutely didn't stop him and we emerged from the theater with pink, blurred faces, a tickled-to-death couple, that he told me on the way home that he really hadn't wanted to start dating me because of my father.

"But you're not him," he said. "Are you?"

I didn't even pause. I didn't resist or explain or defend my family. "No, I'm not," I said. "Definitely not."

I would've said anything to keep him with me, to make sure he didn't change his mind, and perhaps I was lucky he didn't ask anything worse, but that was the beginning for me, and I knew it, of a different life. When I got back inside the apartment, I looked at my mother, who had fallen asleep on the sofa waiting for me, and I thought, *This apartment is really shabby*. And in the room I shared with my sister, I hissed at Barbara when she woke up, "Stop looking at me. I despise your looking at me."

For a long time, I'd held what I thought of as two opinions. With my parents, I was entirely against the war and all wars. What could be gained by millions of people marching out with the sole purpose of killing as many of each other as they could? I couldn't believe this butchery was *allowed*. Had always been allowed. The ugliest of all insanities. I was proud of my father for not going along with any of it. On the other hand, we all saw the photos of the concentration camps in Europe, after our soldiers went in, the living skeletons lying among piles of corpses, and what if our side hadn't won? Could people who did such things ever be stopped by peaceable means? I didn't mind having two viewpoints—it made talking to my friends easier (especially Ruthie), and it showed that I was advanced enough as a thinker to hold more than one idea in my mind at a time. Wasn't that a sign of a higher intelligence?

"It's okay to have two opinions," my mother said, "if all you have to do is have an opinion. If."

I thought my mother, typically, was making everything harder than it had to be. Meanwhile, Ted and I were getting along extremely well. We cracked each other up at the newspaper meetings, we talked about what a bunch of yahoos most of the school was. We argued about whether Tolstoy was better than Dostoyevsky (I said, "Tolstoy is *fuller*") and we agreed about William Dean Howells being really boring. And he walked me between classes at school, a sign of major attention. *This is what real life is*, I thought, at his side in the hallways, *and I have it already*. Even Maxie started being nicer to me.

Once, when I was complaining about a sudden streak of sultry weather in May, Ted said, "My father always liked the heat." I had stopped feeling that he held his father's dying against me, and I had gone over to another feeling, an envy of what Ted knew about death.

"You should like hot weather, then," I said. "As a tribute."

He nodded at this, he liked my making room for his ceremonies of memory.

We did a lot of necking. I was only sixteen, I didn't think—

and he didn't demand—we would get into actual sex, but we hovered in an exquisite border area, became adepts in its every shading of excitement. How slow and patient we were then, how attenuated in our efforts. It was the sweetheart desire of innocents, for all its shocks and grunts and revelations.

He was two years ahead of me in school, and I did not have a good feeling about his graduating, though I gave him a very nice edition of Tolstoy's *Resurrection* for a present. I didn't like the way he thanked me for it by saying, "I only hope I'll have time to read it." He was going to City College, just a subway ride uptown, but I had reason to fear he'd slip away from me.

And I wasn't wrong. He took up with some female from his Western Civ class, and, then more fatally, with a blonde who worked in the library. He decided that we should no longer "fence each other in" and I was "free" to date other people. During this speech, he looked stern and aggrieved at having to speak at all. "Thank you for the blessing of liberty," I said. Sarcasm was not even slightly effective.

What could I do? I wanted to fight for him, fight hard and dirty if I had to. I had my pride and my upbringing, but I wasn't above using Maxie. Nothing sneaky, but I goaded her into inventing mean nicknames (Frog Eyes, Miss Dainty) and using her gifts of mimicry after the poor girlfriend paid a family visit. Maxie claimed the girl had actually said, "I *adore* pot roast," and Maxie loudly adored everything in sight for weeks after.

My job was to be the true blue one. If I ran into him (Maxie aided this), I was friendly, forthright, calm. "Great to see you, Ted. Everything okay?" Ever loyal. Very, very warm.

My mother did not admire my scheming. "What can you gain by trickery?" she said.

"It's not tricks," I said. "And all is fair in love and war."

"Oh, Louise," she said. "Can you hear yourself, can you?"

I spent two years of my adolescence gutted by the outrage of being without him, eaten up with agonized guesses
about my future. It was constantly clear to me what I had
to have, every cell in my body was fixed in certainty. I had
no way to know whether I would win. All the nights of
imagined raptures, could they be for nothing? My friend
Ruthie, who didn't have anything going yet, envied my suffering, and probably thought it was better to have loved
and lost than never to have loved at all, but I didn't. And
I didn't have a plan B. When Ruthie said, "You could get
Alan Brody to like you if you wanted," I said, "No! Thank
you, no." No halfway measures, no compromises. I knew
what I knew. I shouldered my burden, I had been bred to
staunchness.

Senior year I worked after school at a bakery in the neighborhood. It was called Mrs. Plymouth's, a homey place with mile-
high coconut cakes and fudge-filled yellow layers. People still
remembered when butter and sugar had been rationed in the
last war years, and they liked the party-prettiness of what we
sold. My earnings went to our ailing household budget; my
father had found a job at a print shop, but we were always
behind on our bills.

I told my mother I could bring in more money as a file
clerk, once I was out of school. Plenty of girls as smart as I

was had jobs like that, and (I didn't say this) I hoped to get married very soon anyway. Neither of my parents had been to college, but my father had his heart set on my getting a degree, and his bloodied heart was sacred to all of us. My mother thought I should go to Hunter (all girls) and not City, where I would run into we-knew-who.

I ran into him anyway, in the bakery, where he pretended to be surprised to find me. "Hey!" he said. "What's up?"

"Couldn't be better," I said. "This is *such* a good time for me. I think I'm going to Hawaii. To help with the big dock-workers' strike."

"Hawaii! How will you get there?"

"There are ways. I have friends."

"What friends?"

"Oh, you know. So school is good?"

I had been raised to always, always be truthful, and I refused to say more, knowing I was not a skillful liar. "Forget I mentioned it," I said. "Okay? Please."

"Hawaii, huh?" he said.

"Forget I said it." I gave him my sunniest, sweetest look. "Everything good with you?" And I went off to wait on someone else.

I didn't have wiles, not really, but I knew that woe and supplication had no sex appeal. He phoned me that night, trying to find out who I was seeing. I let him talk me out of my fake Hawaii plan, and that was the start of our revival.

No triumph could have been purer, more glorious, than those early days of having him back. I was smug with victory, I went around giving my sister the most platitudinous advice about love and life: "If it's meant to be, it happens," "When you know, you know." His mother was less than pleased about me and tended to refer to my parents as Reds, no matter how many times I explained they were anarchists, not Marxists—the black flag, not the red flag!—and their actions these days were mostly down to picketing with labor unions, which was perfectly lawful. I did go out on picket lines with them (we'd always done this as a family), but I wasn't big on chanting. "They're just slogans!" I said.

"What *do* you have faith in?" my mother said.

The truth was that I wanted to be ordinary. I wanted the coziness of private life. Why should that be out of reach, why couldn't I have that?

"I have faith in *people*," I said.

"What does that mean?" my mother said. "You think you can do without ideas but you can't."

I lasted through a year and a half of college, and then Ted and I were married. It was his idea as much as mine—his dating life had scared him about the risks of ending up with someone shrill or cloying or shallow or stupid. I was at the very least none of those things. Once we were engaged, we had sex of a lavish and reverent kind. He looked at me very intently afterward, his eyes deep in their sockets, without his glasses, and his features softened and slightly swollen, an almost-naked face. I was dazzled myself, but I had been dazzled before we even did anything.

My parents were against my marrying Ted—my mother said, "You're selling yourself to the first bidder," a surprisingly

bitter thing for her to say—but they put together a decent
wedding for me, not fancy but with bouquets of pink carna-
tions and a real cake from the bakery. Everyone was crowded
into our living room, and we had a Unitarian minister, which
satisfied no one, and I wore a dress I'd sewn from a pattern,
with a scalloped neck and a gathered skirt, in dotted swiss,
white on white. I looked good in that dress.

Ted had managed to graduate a semester early, and the
city was in bleak winter. We moved into a tenement on the
Lower East Side, with crappy heating, and I worked very
hard to make it nice. We paid the rent from Ted's new job
teaching English in a high school, and I liked all the budget-
ing and household cleverness.

No one in my family admired the drapes I made for the windows, a tasteful slubbed weave in creamy beige. "I can see a
lot of effort went into this," my mother said, not that nicely.

"Isn't everything you fight for," I said, "the peace and the
fair wages, for the sake of each family?"

"We fight for *freedom*," my sister said. "Not for cornflakes."

But I fooled them all by being happy.

Ted came home every day from being a "permanent sub"
teaching five English classes—oh, God, five—of ninth- and
tenth-graders in deepest Brooklyn, and he could be very
funny. We'd crack up over their misapprehensions of *Silas
Marner* and their hilarious sentences, and I'd get indignant
on his behalf when the principal made absurd decrees, and

in this spirit of teamwork we ate my excellent meals, and by dessert I was explaining why I thought Pearl Buck wasn't that great a writer or how Tolstoy could get into any character's head. I had plenty of time to read.

We were happy in bed too. I had a life of considerable animal pleasures, a day of simple tasks easily done, and a husband who treated me well. I felt very elemental, in our fifth-floor walk-up, with its clanging pipes and lopsided walls—I was a person who'd guessed right about what was essential. I had what I wanted. How many people have that?

I didn't even mind the summer, when our small, boxed-in rooms were airless ovens and we slept on the fire escape. Ted was teaching summer school to make more money, and in the days alone, I'd go dunk myself in the municipal pool on Carmine Street, near where I used to live. The pool was so crowded it was like swimming on the subway, but I'd see Ruthie or other girls I'd known in high school. I felt older, calmer, less worried than they were. I'd lie on a towel in my bathing suit and be very aware that my body was not a virgin's body.

Ted's summer school had all the students who'd flunked, and he was stuck with seventh grade (which he wasn't even licensed for), a nightmarish age. Squirming, untamed creatures. He could not get them interested in the poetry of Oliver Wendell Holmes or the need for verb agreement. They were always talking, eating candy, passing notes, exploding into illicit laughter over who-knew-what.

One evening, Ted said he had worked out a "plan for dominance." He'd told the class that any student who reported on another student eating in class or passing a note would be rewarded with an extra tenth of a point toward his or her grade.

"You're training them to rat on each other?" I said.

"I'm teaching them to be loyal to me above all."

"That's fascism," I said. He laughed.

In my family, ratting was the lowest of the low. My father had survived in prison by not breaking solidarity with other inmates and refusing special favors from the warden, lest people think he was a spy, and in the years since, more than one friend had gone to prison (and not for just a few months either) rather than give names of people who belonged to so-called Communist fronts.

"So you bribe them to turn each other in," I said, "and you're going to give them a false grade, with padded points?"

"You know absolutely nothing about keeping control in the classroom," he said. "You have no idea. Do you?"

Ted came home the next day and said, "Hah! It's working." Three boys were turned in for eating a bag of Tootsie Rolls. He'd sent the three to the principal's office while Ricky, the kid who reported them, crowed in his seat and was full of himself all day.

When the boys came back to class the following day they stole Ricky's shoes, ripped his shirt, and then claimed to find a half-eaten Milky Way on his desk. "Here's the evidence! You said we had to have evidence!"

Ted walked all four of them, whining in protest, to the

principal. All was calm, except the principal came by after school to ask why Ted was having so much trouble.

"Uh-oh," I said.

"I have to think of other punishments."

He had to what? I saw that I didn't know him very well, which made me feel extremely stupid. I hadn't seen him this way before because I hadn't seen him up close when he was losing. He was losing this class, I could tell.

The punishment he "invented" was docking their grades, and the summer became a tournament of shaved points up and down, a tangle of calculations and pettiness and futile warfare. He explained its progress often, and I could never follow what he was saying. I felt sorry for him, with his bluster and his vain efforts. Who was he kidding?

I felt increasingly sorry for me. Not that there was much to do about it, but why did I wait at the end of every day, with dinner on the stove, for a conversation I only wanted to get away from? The system didn't work if I didn't believe in him. Everything seemed ridiculous, including the drapes I'd been so tickled with.

And who did I think I was? Feet of clay, anyone would've said if I had complained about my husband. A mere bump in the long and winding road of marriage. My mother guessed (and I didn't want her to guess), I could tell by the way she peered at me and patted my hand. I told my mother I wasn't pregnant, if that's what she was worried about.

We were still having sex, and I didn't hate the sex either. It was now a more private set of excitements, as if I were crying out to myself. What a liar I was becoming, on all counts, scared and selfish both. Ted half knew, but only half. Some women stayed in love with their husbands long after the men began to beat them or cheat on them or publicly shame them. Ted was hardly guilty of anything worse than being a new and incompetent teacher. I knew that, I told myself that.

Once summer school was over, Ted had a brief spell of holiday in the hottest part of August. He dragged a kitchen chair out to the fire escape and sat in his undershirt, reading. Didn't he want to go to the beach? Maybe just uptown to Central Park? He didn't want to do anything. "What's the point?" he said. He read the newspapers all day, he read magazines written for stupider people. "Go swim with your friends," he said. "I'm fine here."

When the pool closed for its annual week of maintenance, I sat with Ted on the fire escape, but he didn't want any chatting. And he didn't want the radio blaring from the kitchen either. No Tchaikovsky, no Fats Domino. "I guess that job really made you tired," I said.

"What do you care?" he said.

I had brought about this state of irritated sorrow, this defeat. He did know.

I'd always been taught the truth sets you free, but it wasn't doing that here. Here was a man who could hardly move from the weight of the truth. His sweating body was hunched over the page as he read. Hours passed when he didn't raise his head. Who had made him suffer? I wanted to punch this person in the nose.

"Didn't you used to fish in the park with your dad?" I said. "Don't you want to go to the lake sometime?"

"I bet your dad never fished. I bet he didn't want to kill a single minnow."

"Anarchists *used* to be very violent, some of them. My father is an evolved form."

"Why didn't you marry him, then?"

I gasped and stared at him. "Very funny," I said.

"You think he's this great hero," Ted said. "But he let my father die. He didn't help him."

I was furious then at Ted's father, who'd been killed at Anzio—a playful man with boorish tendencies, in Ted's stories. It was just as well I had nothing to say against him because I might've said it. A decade had passed, a whole other inexplicable war had happened since then—the "action" in Korea was just over that summer—what was making Ted bring this up now?

"What do you want from me?" I said.

"Admit he's a failure."

"Who?"

"Your father."

"Failed how?" I said.

"To do anything. Ever."

"Like what?"

"Did he stop the war by getting arrested? Did he bring an end to all governments?"

"It isn't *about* that," I said.

"It's all gestures," he said. "Showing off."

"It is not."

"You sit on your can all day and you think you know about the real world, but you don't."

"Who do you think you're talking to?"

"The queen of fake purity."

I went inside the apartment to get away from him, and then I kept going, out the door, down the five flights to the street. How far away could I get? The street had the summer smell of ripe garbage and incinerated soot. Our sweltering block was at its quietest, with all the Jewish shops shuttered for Saturday, but on one stretch of sidewalk the Puerto Rican kids were playing, yelling and chasing each other and calling out dares. I'd made a great mistake in marrying Ted. Nothing could be clearer. What was I going to do now? I walked east, block after faded-brick block, till I got to where the streets ended, and past the bank of seared grasses, the glaring water of the river rose like a mirage. I'd fought so hard to get him. There were clues all along but I'd had no use for them, I might've paid attention but I didn't want to. I thought the world was love-love-love.

And if I left his bed and board, how would I live? Back to the bakery? I was so dazed and stricken that I sat thinking about Boston cream pie and peanut butter cookies, soothing thoughts, brainless dreams, until the fading light scared me and I walked home.

When I got back to the apartment, Ted was lying in bed, facedown. He turned when I came in. "If you want to leave, just leave," he said. "You can go back to your parents. That's the simplest thing."

How reasonable he sounded, how hoarse and desperate.

I could be free in an instant if I wanted to be. As I was taking this in, I heard myself crying, loud as an infant; I made horrible sounds of real anguish. "Don't make me leave," I managed to say. How choked and pathetic my voice was. I said weepy things about how I loved him, I said we were meant for each other and he knew it too, didn't he?—I knew he did. The words flew out of me, as if they were true. Was I lying? The whole time I was speaking, I felt that I had to put this over, I had to act with as much conviction as I could. Did I believe it? I did and I didn't.

And I made Ted happy. Under my wails and moans and tears, he softened. His eyes lost their stunned, dead look and took on their old, intelligent shimmer. I was pulling us back from a very dangerous precipice. We could be safe, we could be. A bliss of relief went through both of us.

All that suffering had a good effect on us in bed, as if we had been through a battle together as comrades, not enemies. Our natures were more fully bared to each other. We had only to take off our clothes to be our more audacious, less naïve selves. We knew more, we went further. It startled us both, and we laughed in astonishment after.

When Ted went back to school in September, he was given an extra class—could his day be any fuller?—and I was outraged for him, which he liked. When he had to appear at Meet the Teachers Night, I decided to be eager to be in the audience. I sat with other wives in the big wood-and-linoleum auditorium, surrounded by a sea of parents, while our spouses stood and explained their educational goals. Ted said he hoped to bring students to an understanding of the power of the English language. A Mr. Sloan, whose wife was next to me, said he believed that algebra refined all thinking. "Well, they have to say *something*," she whispered.

"Or take the Fifth," I said. A Latin teacher in the school had been fired for taking the Fifth Amendment when asked about Communists in the Teachers Union, and I suddenly thought this was not my best joke. Not funny to me. But the woman smiled.

"At least they're not talking about locking the bad students in the closet," she murmured. "They used to do that when I was a kid."

"Some of them need it now."

"I'll say," she said.

"My husband bribes them to rat on each other," I said. "He gives them rewards for it."

"Does he?" she said.

Someone shushed us, and I flinched in my seat—it was right to shut me up. What sort of person had I become now, with spite leaking out of me? If Ted had started baiting and buying off his ninth-graders, what did it matter to me? I had to hope she would forget my words, why would she bother to remember, and I got away from Mrs. Sloan when we all filed into the gym for punch and cookies. "You were excellent," I said to Ted.

"Aw, shucks," he said.

• • •

But I knew what I was. At the slightest opportunity, at the first instant that offered, I'd informed on my husband, just like that. Speaking against him had been very easy. Every day people were hounded for refusing to bear witness against someone—they were fired or arrested or blacklisted for being un-American and still they kept their mouths shut, on principle. And me? I leaped at the chance to spread a small bit of damage about the man I slept with every night.

Mr. Sloan was, in fact, the vice principal, I later found out. This was not good news. Ted was on a one-year contract, and if they dropped him, what school would take him? I had never been like this before I knew Ted. Who knew what I would blurt out next? *Look what love has done to me*, I thought.

One night, after we'd had perfectly good sex and Ted fell asleep and I lay awake for hours, it struck me with horror that I had never been a good liar but now I was. I could scarcely take off my clothes and turn to my husband without some degree of fraudulence and calculation. I, who'd been raised to be always truthful, had somehow taught myself to be one of those women who lure and lie for their survival. How had this happened? *This is what gives carnal relations a bad name*, I thought, as if I could joke to myself about it.

Maybe all marriages, if you looked too hard at them, were riddled with corrupting compromises. Maybe other people had a higher tolerance for the bargains they struck, and that was just the way of it. I was going to have to live with this particular insight. It wasn't something I wanted to shout from the rooftops to anyone. I had a long, bad night, with Ted's steady breathing next to me in the bed and the noise of trucks going by in the street below. In the books I liked to read, and in the politics of my parents, people changed once they got hold of a new way to see things, but I wasn't going to change. I wasn't.

In the spring Ted got official word that his contract wasn't being renewed. No reason was given—they would only say another teacher was filling the spot—and a number of people thought it was because my parents were Communists, even if they weren't. Someone said the vice principal had been especially against Ted. I was so upset I could barely tell people, my voice broke when I gave the news—while Ted, to my complete surprise, went in for cheerful irony. "We don't need to eat, what's so great about eating?" he said, and "I love a character-building experience," and (his favorite), "Exploited today, fired tomorrow."

How little I knew him. This wisenheimer flintiness, this hearty valor, was not at all what I might have expected. I was the vile, small-minded, petty, treacherous one. I was the one who had burned our ticket to a decent, straightforward life. And now I gave long speeches about how we lived in tainted times, and how all the higher-ups were jealous of Ted's star teaching. "Hey," Ted said. "We'll get by. Not the end of the world." He comforted me, my husband who'd been robbed.

What could I do? I kept seeking him out in bed, trying to lavish myself on him and to dower him with oblivion. I hardly let him rest, I kept drawing him back and wanting to begin again. It seemed the very least I could contribute to our dreary situation. The spell of it worked on me too; I'd emerge still half delirious, bruised and spent, out of myself. I whispered to him, "Best of all husbands."

"You're my girl."

"They have no idea who you really are," I said.

"Forget 'them,'" he said. "Nobody's here. Just us."

In our room, a single light flickered from a candle I'd set by the bed.

"My father's a failure," I said.

"What?"

"He is."

"Why are you saying that?"

"I want to."

"Shush," he said. "Be calm, okay? It's all right."

If he no longer wanted to hear any such thing, there were other things he wanted. He wanted complete silence while he read for hours, he wanted to win any argument about any topic, from Tolstoy's translators to the post-armistice in Korea, and I let him. When my parents fed us nourishing suppers, he kept up his darkly blithe quips about his prospects. "Exploited today, fired tomorrow," he said (yet again). They all laughed. They liked him better now. My sister said, "I wish you were a teacher in *my* school." My father poured beer for him and talked to him about purges and backlash and touched his shoulder, which Ted seemed to like. He didn't, after all, have a father of his own.

· · ·

But what were we going to do and what about me? My mother let me use the typewriter in her office to tap out Ted's job-seeking letters to states where he wasn't known. What a mess I had made. Ted's paychecks stopped in June.

I told him I was going to ask if they needed anyone at the bakery, and I was a little surprised when he didn't object. It was humbling to return to Mrs. Plymouth's as a married woman—"Didn't think we'd see *you*," customers said—but I still liked the buttery smells, the doilies on glass shelves, even the striped aprons and the silly hairnets, that orderly, sugary version of home.

My mother said there was no dishonor in being short of cash. "*Au contraire*," Barbara said. I brought home crumbled cookies and soggy Danish that stuffed Ted and me and made us feel poorer.

Ted suggested I bring boxes of day-old cake to the Ramirez family down the hall, and their kids adored us after that. I liked my poor husband better than I ever had. He was oddly improved by being broken—I'd read of that happening, but I'd never seen it before in real life. He told Maxie, "I couldn't pick a better girl than Louise to be unemployed with."

But I told Ruthie I wasn't, actually, sure I could get through this part on love alone. I was having a Popsicle with her in the park, near a grassy patch we'd always liked. "What if I have to follow him into exile in Siberia?" I said. Ted had just sent an application to Provo, Utah, which we could not resist calling the Steppes.

"You would ditch him when he was down?" she said. Nobody we knew did that. In Hollywood, in trashy magazines, but not in our neighborhoods.

"No," I said. "But I'd hang on without my heart in it. I'd be one of those sour wives, all martyred and sarcastic."

"*No*. Not you. You love Ted," Ruthie said. She had a boyfriend now and hoped their dating would end in marriage, and I was alarming her.

I thought of my mother saying, "Sold to the first bidder," when she wanted to warn me against leaping too fast into love. But if love didn't make the world go around, what did?

A month later, I found myself packing, not for Utah but for Okinawa. The one job that came through for Ted was teaching English to American kids on an air force base in Japan. Ted said all the Americans liked it over there, and there were thousands of Americans still in Japan. With children who needed my husband's attention. My mother was very upset.

"You'll be living *inside* the U.S. military," she said. "Do you want that? You don't want that."

"I'll learn Japanese!" I said. Although they said people hardly left the base, I dreamed of myself making new sounds. "I have to be with my husband," I told her.

"He doesn't have to go."

I wanted to go. I felt superior to everyone I knew because I was going.

"You stuck with Dad," I said.

"Do I have to say how different that was?"

My father didn't say much, but he was clearly very disappointed. He'd look into my face and then turn his gaze away.

Did I have no principles at all? My sister said, "Do you know where you're going? They used to send planes from out of there to bomb Korea. For Christ's sake."

Ted and I were in wonderful spirits. Japan! We talked for hours about what to bring, we read *The Chrysanthemum and the Sword* and a book of haiku the library had. I found a recipe for sukiyaki and I stirred bits of beef in a pan with canned bean sprouts. "Sometimes bad luck turns into good luck," Ted said. We both thought we'd fallen into a wildly suitable fate: everything would be taken care of, and everything would be beyond what we'd imagined. We were making a great escape. We fell asleep holding hands.

My sister said, "I never thought you would be like this."

We were going by ship from California, and we had to send everything in trunks and crates. What was the weather like? Like here in the rest of Japan but warmer in Okinawa. And I read that the Japanese believed theirs was the only country that really had four seasons, which seemed sweet of them. I was sorting out which books to give to Ruthie when Ted came into the room, shouting, "I don't believe it!" Papers had come with an official seal: Ted had a security clearance to reside on the base, but family member Louise Buckman Pfeiffer was refused one.

"Did you know about this?" I wailed.

I'd never heard of such a thing. But what, really, had I heard of?

"Maybe I can get work as a janitor in your bakery," Ted said grimly.

I hated the goddamn government. My parents were right. Had always been right. "You should go without me," I said. I was angry with Ted for having wanted to go in the first place. "You should just go as if you really were in the army."

Ted was hugging me. "You're the most amazing person." We were both sticky from the summer heat, and the scent of his skin was such a sharp, familiar smell as he held me.

He was ready to get on the ship to Japan without me, and he thought I was noble. I felt crazy.

I could have stopped him from going, but I didn't. He kept saying, "There aren't many wives like you," as if I were a paragon of enlightened sacrifice. "I am just so wonderful," I said, but he didn't mind my tone. Why should he mind? He was going to have his adventure. I was the one cheated and defeated. Ted, in those last weeks, seemed to have decided he had a treasure in me. He'd watch me move around the house and say, "You are something." He'd hold me close for minutes at a time, and I'd feel my heart in my chest beating for him. He would miss me. I was scared and said so, but he thought this was another sign of my valor.

The first months without him were atrocious. I had to move back to my parents' apartment, and I'd lie awake in my old room, with Barbara rustling around in the next bed, and everything was intolerable. The absence of Ted was like a weight in all my limbs, and my poor body was beset with useless longing. Ted made one expensive phone call to me on arrival—"The base is ugly!" he said, and sounded very thrilled. It was three weeks before a letter reached me (*When I take walks I see water buffalo in the fields! Also lots of geckos and mosquitos. The students are easy—I don't have to bribe them!*), and I wrote to him every day (*The autumn weather is still very warm* and *Barbara wants to be a French major, very practical*). My father said, "I can't get over having a son-in-law on a military base," and in truth I agreed with him. The whole thing was a humiliation.

My work at the bakery was not very taxing and the hours felt very, very long. I ate too many cupcakes. My mother suggested I bring some of those eternal leftovers to the Catholic Worker place on Chrystie Street, which their friend Dorothy ran. Dorothy wasn't there most of the time, and the House of Hospitality was full of old winos and young crazies, wacky, life-damaged people, roaming the rooms of an old building, with crucifixes on the walls looking down on all of it. They were exactly the people no one else wanted to bother with. Everybody—staff and residents alike—was thrilled by the boxes of pastries. "It's Louise!" they would yell, when I walked in the door. One woman jumped around in circles until she had to be calmed by someone.

What did I ever believe? My mother used to say my politics were driven out by my hormones, an insulting version of my history. Serious thought, as well as lust, had made it plain to me that love was truer than all the other weak notions in the world, and that justice could never be served by anything you did (what was the use?), so there was no satisfaction serving it. Now I was in a different spot.

Ted wrote, *I wish wish wish you were here.* Well, I wasn't. His contract was for two years, and he had one free trip home in a year. How could I be lost in bedroom fantasies of someone I was so outraged with? At the bakery I had a hazy, distracted look a lot of the time, too much of the time. We were paid very little, and some of the women had families living on this pay. "Wake up, Susie-Q," they would say to me.

Ted thought I was being "rash and shortsighted" when I moved out of my rent-free home with my family and got a one-room apartment on East Third Street—tub in the kitchen, toilet in the hall. "By yourself?" Ruthie said. "No one else?"

My mother said, "I thought you wanted to save money."

Nobody thought I was smart, and maybe they were right. But how many months could I stay in my old room with Barbara? I tried very hard to make the new place interesting, I worked on the décor—the one wall painted coral-orange, the poster of Picasso's *Guernica*, with its twisted figures. I was not really at home there at first, but I thought that I would be, and I was right. I'd been raised to love freedom (of another sort, but this sort had a meaning) and my pride took me a long way. Sometimes the sight of my own table, where I read whatever I wanted to while I ate, put me in a kind of rapture. No one believed me.

• • •

At Thanksgiving, my father took all of us to join a small march downtown in support of the United Auto Workers' strike at the Kohler steel plant in Wisconsin. My mother brought a thermos of hot cider to make sure Barbara and I stayed warm. The Thanksgiving weather was sunny and not so cold and we knew a lot of the people marching, so it was a fairly festive afternoon. BE WISE, DON'T BUY KOHLER PLUMB-ING SUPPLIES, my picket sign said.

And how was Ted's holiday, with his fellow Americans in Japan? Not bad, but he missed me. His voice sounded under-water when he called. He got to go to the Officers' Club, where they all drank enormous amounts of whiskey and sang "Over the Meadow and Through the Woods" together. A staff sergeant kept imitating a turkey. Gobble, gobble. Yes, yes, I missed him, but I was secretly glad I wasn't there.

And so it went. We longed for each other in raging fevers and we nursed our resentments. My youth was being wasted, and Ted said he was in exile because of my parents. Clearly he kind of liked his exile. (*Just tried local noodles. With stewed pig's feet!* he wrote. *Very tasty!*) To distract myself, I went and took a night course at Hunter College, Love and Money in the Victorian Novel. I was older now and spoke more in class, I had opinions about Becky Thatcher.

Arigato meant "thank you" in Japanese, Ted wrote, and *konnichiwa* was hello. In the spring Ted was coaching a school softball team. I'd never seen the man play baseball in my life. We stopped squabbling in our phone calls but I didn't always know what he was talking about. I was friendly with two girls from my class at Hunter and we'd go for tea afterward and have ideas about Rochester's blindness. And then how nice it was to come back to my room, the stillness at the end of the night. Ted was in my thoughts but it wasn't so bad being parted. I could tell he felt that too.

"How'd you come up with this?" he said, when he saw my apartment, on his big trip home in August. We'd already embraced long and hard at the door, but he was a little thrown by the coral-orange wall and the desolate sink. "*I* like it," I said. I was still tasting the feel of his mouth, the fresh surprise of it. "I pictured something different," he said.

But we did very well, in our odd circumstances. Once we got over a few preliminaries in bed, we were back as familiars, lolling in the luxury of actually really having each other. I had forgotten the Ted-ness of sex with him, the specificity of it. All my craving had not been a true memory. How weak the imagination was.

Ted said, "In Japan they take baths at night, they think we're weird with our showers in the morning." He enjoyed slipping in these reports. I was curious, but not as curious as he thought. "They eat raw horse meat, not just raw fish, can you believe it?" he said. "But they're very clean. The base is immaculate." My friendly imperialist of a husband. I didn't talk much about school, I didn't want to hear what he thought he knew about Dickens.

The clock was ticking, we only had two weeks to be happy

together. It took concentration, but we did all right. I cried at the airport—I felt so bad for myself—but I said, "Don't mind me, I'm silly," as if I really were a soldier's wife.

At the bakery, one of the older women teased me about those geishas over there and how the smart thing would be to have a little bundle of joy to keep him tied to home. People really said these things? I couldn't tell her: *I love my husband and I don't.* And everybody knows, you can't be a little bit pregnant.

I'd long since lapsed out of writing letters every day, and in the second year I didn't always remember every week. When his monthly checks arrived, I'd write, *Thank you for your lovely contribution to the ever-popular Louise Likes to Eat Fund.* I did need them for the rent. Was this what made us married, that he still sent me money? Sometimes he'd say, *I know you can always use it*, as if it were extra. *I love your taste in check-book paper*, I wrote. *The green tint goes with everything.*

I had a preposterous flirtation with one of the bakers on the night shift at Mrs. Plymouth's—he came on during my last hour of work, and sometimes we kidded around in the kitchen. His name was Trevor, he was from Trinidad, and I told him he looked like Harry Belafonte. (He did.) He was very careful around me, but when I complimented him on his way with the dough he gave me an appropriately merry look. My fantasies of him began to block out my fantasies of Ted, which was a peculiar feeling. And what did it matter, if it was all in my head anyway? But one evening I asked Trevor what his days were like, did he sleep all day, and I somehow invited him for supper on Monday, when the bakery was closed.

He dressed so nicely for that dinner, in a pressed shirt of dazzling pale blue, and we talked about the winters in Trinidad—"Oh, yes, gets up past eighty degrees"—over my fried flounder and mashed potatoes. "I like the colors in your house," he said. "Little, little place but you make it pretty."

I had to give him a sign—I brushed against him on the way to the stove—and after that it was simple. We were in bed! I'd never thought I would have any other lover but Ted, and I was astonished at myself, even after all the rehearsals in my mind. He was different from Ted—more full of flourishes, and also more jolly and confident. I thought that I was a reckless person but I had chosen a kind man. *I can do this*, I thought, *I'm lucky*.

This went on for several months, although Trevor was always afraid he was going to be fired if the bakery found out. This was perfectly true—we didn't have a union—and we both knew what hideous strains of ugliness might be waiting for him. We rarely talked about race, that most delicate of topics.

"Happy but going nowhere," he said of us.

"I know, I know," I said.

We never went outside together, we never went anywhere except my place. The kids in the building tittered at us in the hall and sometimes worse. They were just kids but I hated them. We kept ourselves out of sight, like the scandal we were.

"You know what I have in Trinidad, near Port-of-Spain?" he said one night.

"No," I said.

"You know. A wife."

Why are you telling me this? I hadn't known but I wasn't stunned for more than a minute. I had a husband, didn't I?

"Her name is Hyacinth," he said.

This was not a good sign, that he wanted to invoke her by name. Some dopey little girl of a wife, who sat home in a tiny kitchen all day, waiting for his MoneyGrams.

"That's how it is," he said.

Oh, was it? He wanted me to let him go before there was trouble for either of us. He wanted me to be a good sport.

"Time to call it a day, isn't it?" I said.

"I am so sorry," he said. He did have manners.

In the bakery, for weeks after, we hardly spoke when we passed each other. When we moved around the kitchen and made sure our gazes didn't meet, I felt that life had insulted us both. I tried not to hear his voice in the room, the tune of his English.

One evening I didn't see him on his shift, and one of the counter girls said he'd left for another job. "When?" I said. "When did he go?" None of them had the name of where he'd gone—"How would I know?" they said—and I couldn't keep asking every single person.

Ruthie said, "Is your heart broken? I'm worried about you."

"I would say no. Not broken. Do I look devastated to you?" I said. "A little the worse for wear maybe."

"Do you have a heart?" Ruthie said. "Just kidding."

• • •

Ted wrote, *And you know what is interesting about the Japanese? Their single-mindedness at any task. How purely they concentrate. I like their sake too!*

It wasn't really that much of a surprise, near the end of the second year, when Ted began to say in his letters that he might be staying on. What did I think? *What kind of man wants to live on an air base?* I thought. I still thought of Trevor every day, but I'd gotten sort of interested in a guy I'd talked to about getting a union into the bakery. He worked for the CIO, traveling to their member unions, and was on the road all the time. We hadn't done more than have conversations, but he called from Duluth and Sioux Falls and told me goofy jokes. So it was clear that life had possibilities. *If you really feel you're needed there,* I wrote to Ted.

You are such a rare wife, Ted wrote. *This is hard on both of us but I will be getting a raise and sending a little more money.*

"How can he keep you on ice like that?" Ruthie said. I thought Ted probably had a Japanese woman in town or maybe some secretary on the base, somebody he wasn't about to marry. I wasn't angry at him for this. I told people he was staying because the salary kept getting higher, and sometimes I said it was because his work was so rewarding.

My mother said, "It's very unusual."

"Is that a crime?" I said. "Unusualness? I thought you were on the side of that."

• • •

Ted came back in July that year, in time for Ruthie's wedding. I had to bring him, I couldn't leave him home. There we were, sitting together in the synagogue, with Ruthie in white silk organza marching toward this Bob guy she was so crazy about. It made me as tearful as it made everyone else, at the same time I felt it was all a poufy fraud. Why would you vow yourself to an unlikely ideal? I snuck a look at Ted, dressed up in a navy-blue suit I'd never seen, and to my amazement he took my hand. We had been getting along at home but not saying much. Now he was rubbing my fingers, an old sweet gesture. *He's grateful to me*, I thought.

So it went. Once he was gone, I did take up with Mick, the union organizer, who was really a very charming guy and never in town for more than a month at a time. He was used to talking to all kinds of people, and once you got him off his rhetoric, he had great stories. The guy whose dog always knew what time it was, the woman who sang in two languages at once: Mick could tell you about all of it.

He was very taken with me, and he didn't like it when I neglected him for my night classes or my homework, but I pretty much stuck to my guns. He'd say, "Sweetie, just tonight," and I could say, not too meanly, "Honey, I'm not your wife." Ted paid the rent, such as it was, and I had no reason to take off my wedding ring. I had the protection of a husband without the nuisance of him being there. Everybody thought I was kidding myself.

• • •

Meanwhile, Mick and I, after a lot of work, got the Bakery and Confectionery Workers International Union voted into Mrs. Plymouth's, much to the disgust of the burly old owner. (Mrs. Plymouth was a fiction.) The owner was very disappointed in me and would've fired me if he could've (not legal!), but I was leaving then anyway, because I'd actually managed to graduate from college.

My mother wanted to make me a dress to wear to commencement, a touching but terrible idea. My father was immensely pleased. One of his kittens was getting a diploma. "We did okay, didn't we?" he kept saying. Mick, who was not a secret from my family, sat with him at graduation. They were great pals.

Ted wrote, *Congratulations to my brilliant wife.*

I got a silly English-major's job as a proofreader at a women's magazine, where I read pap all day ("twenty smart tricks with paper towels") and was good at finding mistakes about baking, which I did know about. My proofreading skills catapulted me into a much better job at the National Maritime Union (okay, Mick knew someone), where I copyedited their newsletter and eventually sort of rewrote most of it and was, in time, listed on the masthead as an editor.

And what about Ted? When I moved to a better apartment, he wrote, *Don't make it so nice I don't recognize it.* How long could this go on? *Have unpacked your favorite sheets*, I wrote, *and they lie waiting for you*. Ted wrote, *Miss those sheets like crazy*. Did I mind that Ted didn't come home that year? I thought I did. He said he was saving his money to improve his housing, or something like that. He stayed faithful in his monthly allotments to me, whatever that meant. Mick wasn't around then either—he was working in Idaho for a few months—and it was a long, bleak summer. "Don't take this personally," Ruthie said, "but I think you're an idiot."

"It's okay now, but what if you get sick?" my mother said. "Later on, I mean. What if you need help and there's no one?" My health stood every chance of staying excellent for a while, Mick had once made me a hot toddy when I had a cold, and we all knew women lived longer than men anyway. "Someday," my mother said, "you're going to have to decide."

Lots of people at the Maritime Union knew Mick, but my name was still Mrs. Pfeiffer to them. I never lied about any of my life, when asked, and because of that I was considered very frank and outspoken. Imagine that. The job suited me—the old thuggish union guys in their rumpled suits, the seamen getting their papers, the no-nonsense women in the office. And every day I was glad to have something to do with keeping the boot of heedless profit off the necks of workers. The newsletter was a little hokey, but I did my best.

• • •

A number of people pointed out that I wasn't going to be young forever, but I was young for a really long time. Mick and I went hiking in the Grand Canyon, and another year we went snowshoeing in Utah, which turned out to be a handsome state. Mick, who'd once worked as what my mother called a "stevedore," tended to like physical stuff. I liked it more than I expected, and for a while I even took ice-skating classes at a rink on a roof in midtown. *You always surprise me*, Ted wrote. *I'm thinking of you in a little twirly skirt.*

I wear slacks, I wrote.

Okinawa was subtropical and never got below fifty. Ted claimed to miss the snow but I didn't believe him.

Well into my thirties, people thought I looked much younger. Ruthie's kids called me Aunt LouLou, as if I were a cartoon auntie. They loved coming to my apartment—much bigger than the last, with blue-painted floors and *Guernica* replaced by a Matisse—but they could never believe I lived alone. No one else here, really? I wasn't just making up a story?

What I didn't like, actually, was when Mick showed up out of nowhere without letting me know in advance. "I have rules," I said, but he ignored them. I was always glad for the sight of him, so I gave way, but it leaked out in other ways, my sense of injustice. We'd quarrel over how much hamburger to buy or which store was a rip-off or who was really a very self-centered person.

Once I had to announce to him that Ted, my husband, was showing up again in August. Ted only came back to the States every few years and he stayed with me when he did. It was, as they say, a given. And Mick had to know to keep away. How difficult was that?

"I think you're telling me to go jump in the lake," Mick said. "Very friendly."

One remarkable thing about Ted was that he never seemed any different, no matter how much time went by. Oh, there was always a moment when I was surprised at how old he looked, and he'd start in about things I'd totally forgotten from his last visit, but we got used to each other at once. We'd hop into bed right away (the same bed, with the maple headboard), and then we'd lie around having a conversation we might have begun only the day before. He'd hold my hand and stroke my fingers. "Hey, Louise," he'd say. "What's up?" It was all very sentimental.

Ruthie was always asking me, "Does he just think he owns you?"

She knew I'd been brought up with much talk about property—property is theft, it's the exploitation of the weak by the strong. "What you really mean," I said, "is that I should exert my ownership rights on *him*. Reel him back in, make him mine."

"You could." Maybe.

"For freedom there is no substitute, there can be no substitute," I said. It was an old quote from Rudolf Rocker, an anarcho-syndicalist my father loved. I didn't think it was all that interesting or true—it was a slogan!—but it had become true for me. Or true sometimes. My mother would've cringed at that qualifier. I used to always tell my parents I was *not* an idealogue. "So what are you?" my mother would say.

"Not a hypocrite."

"That's minimal," my mother said. "That's not an answer." But I thought it was. I liked how I'd turned out. Through trial and error.

When I was close to forty, I had a major quarrel with Mick, about the usual. He wanted me to fly out to see him in St. Louis for a four-day weekend. "I happen to be employed," I said. "I can't just take off."

"I'm paying, darlin'," he said. "It's on me."

"So? Please. Not the point."

"You know what it is?" he said. "I'm the one you don't take seriously."

A man I saw five or six times a year was talking about serious?

"If your hubby wagged his finger to invite you to Japan, you'd hop on a plane and go."

"I don't want to go to Japan! I don't!" I mostly didn't, not anymore.

"St. Louis is a great town. Got the Arch, got the Cardinals. Only needs you."

And I went for those four days, to placate him. St. Louis was fine, but right away he pestered me about staying an extra day, and I got indignant about the sneakiness of that. Why would I neglect my newsletter for him? It was not a good trip, and Mick started to call less often after that.

But Mick didn't disappear altogether. In the middle of the night he'd need to talk to me, or I'd let him slip over when he was in town. So I wasn't entirely single. My solitude had a flavor to it, a tint of distant admiration. It wasn't bad getting those phone calls out of nowhere, kisses on the line. Then I'd stay up late, reading in bed, with his company in the air around me but a pure silence in the room. My room.

Ted was not really that old when he decided to sort of "retire" from his teaching career in Okinawa and set himself up over there as a private tutor of English. He could make a decent amount by the hour and he was looking forward, he said, to living in Japan in a different way. It was really not that expensive for an American to get by, and he would continue sending money home, but less money.

He didn't exactly ask what I thought. Really, the amount he mailed had not changed much over the years and was by now pretty puny. My own salary had moved forward by the usual decent increments, so the change wouldn't break me, would it? My mother was hotly outraged and would've sued him if she'd believed in governments. She actually said, "He owes you more."

Ted was moving into the town and out of the gated and guarded base (which my mother always said sounded like a prison). I sent him a set of curtains for his new house, a very sharp geometric print I thought he would like. I didn't entirely know what he liked anymore but I knew something.

Afterward I worried that I'd picked the wrong fabric. "You are so weird," Ruthie said. "Go buy yourself a new sofa instead."

We were on the phone at the time, and I looked around at my apartment. I liked everything in it, from the floor I had painted a clever shade of blue to the chrome lamp to the bowl of oranges glowing on the table. I was secretly enchanted with my own cruddy décor and its history. What did I need? Nothing wrong with my sofa, which had been in my parents' living room. My stubborn dear parents. You don't know what you're going to be faithful to in this world, do you? It was true I didn't have what other people had, I knew that, and yet I couldn't think of a single other life I envied—no, I couldn't—though I knew better than to try to get anyone to believe it.

Better

Marcus kept thinking the memoir would make a great movie. He was reading a faded hardback, printed in 1952, with pages that cracked if you dog-eared them, but he couldn't keep away from it. He was lying in a hammock in the yard of his friends' house near Woodstock, and he had found the book on a living room shelf, where it had probably been for the last sixty years. The house had been in Casey's family since forever.

The book was called *Village Days and Nights* and was about radicals and anarchists in Manhattan in the twenties and thirties arguing their brains out and fucking each other's wives. The writing had hokey spots, but Marcus was into it. What a mix of poignant overconfidence (the revolution of the future! the inevitable death of capitalism!—not phrases you heard much in the twenty-first century) and truly sneaky hanky-panky. The author's snarky wife was a great part for somebody.

Marcus agreed with most of what the author said— property *was* theft—but in the same way he believed that Jesus was God Incarnate, which he actually did believe, sort of. These ideas took up a separate sacred space in the mind. Living them out was a bloody mess, you could see from history. That was the problem, wasn't it? He liked the book's company and stayed with it for hours.

When he came in for dinner, he told Casey and Carol, his friends, that he'd found a sure way to make a million bucks. "Uh-oh," Casey said. "I hear next year's bankruptcy talking."

"Gimme a wad and I'll make you rich in Hollywood," Marcus said. He showed them the book, said, "Big biopic," and they knew he was kidding. No more fortunes in the faded glamour of the Left. Too bad. They were all lawyers, and not of the high-revenue kind. Marcus did tenant law, and Casey and Carol (man and wife) worked in immigration law.

And maybe he didn't want to share the book with the world. He was happy with it showing exclusively in the theater of his head. People wouldn't get it, they'd laugh in the wrong spots. His ex-boyfriend had accused Marcus of thinking that about everything: that he was the only one who understood. Also of being withdrawn and emotionally stingy. Marcus was still furious at the injustice of that, which didn't keep him from wanting Nico back.

Casey and Carol had been especially nice to him this weekend—sometimes too nice—to console him for Nico's defection. Tonight they were barbecuing corn and beautifully marinated chicken and slices of watermelon, which they claimed was good grilled, to distract Marcus from his sorrow. He ate heartily but without what you would call feeling. They sat near the glow of the briquettes, swatting away mosquitoes and watching the fireflies, as darkness fell, and then he was glad to slip away to his room and go back inside *Village Days and Nights*.

He'd reached a point in the book where the narrator suspected his wife, Betsy, was sleeping with one of the men in the big group-apartment they shared on Greenwich Avenue. Was she fooling around with Richard ("a Jew from Cincinnati"—the author was not above bigotry) or with Joe ("bland and married and always a cipher")? The author, in his suffering, resorted to taking his hard-to-please wife to a local speakeasy and staying out late, to avoid coming back to the apartment. His wife was lively there and showed enthusiasm for these nights out and he began to see some hope.

The flaw in this plan was that it was draining his meager budget. The author was a badly paid journalist for what now would be called the alternate press. He borrowed money from any friends he could, including Richard and Joe, his suspected cuckolders. And when he was down to nothing, the bar owner let him run a tab, for months and months. The narrator was not proud of this. "Money was its usual false friend to me. How gay my wife was, quaffing her cocktails and smiling at all and sundry."

Marcus was always startled to read *gay* in its old meaning of carefree. This could only strike him with irony at the moment. "My darling Betsy was becoming something of a gold-digger," the author wrote, "though she may not have known it herself. Gandhi said, 'Earth provides enough to satisfy every man's need, but not every man's greed.'"

Gandhi? How did Gandhi get in there? Marcus was amused to think of the Mahatma hanging out in some saloon on Bleecker Street. In fact, he would have been getting ready to lead the great Salt March in India at the time. Marcus was a big Gandhi fan. Could the author have been reading him as early as that? Maybe. Marcus imagined the wounded young husband bolstered by the words of one skinny, bald, half-toothless guy from Gujarat who hadn't had sex with his wife for decades (even then). It made him want to take up Gandhi again himself.

Marcus got up very early the next morning and actually checked the living room bookshelves for Gandhi. *The Story of My Experiments with Truth*, wasn't that here somewhere? In between old Agatha Christie paperbacks and *Steal This Book* by Abbie Hoffman? It was not. Casey's great-uncle had been a painter—the house was full of his splashy landscapes—but the remnants of everyone who'd been here were pretty random.

And now people were saying maybe Gandhi had been in love with a man, a Jewish architect in South Africa. Or at least vice versa. One or both of them had languished in the same sorrow Marcus was getting to know so well. Maybe. Marcus didn't quite buy it. Gandhi had been so busy creating other forms of suffering for himself. Fasting beyond endurance, marching, getting jailed. With such fixity of purpose. But the Great Soul might have had room for everything.

In college, where Marcus was one of a very small group of African-American students, he'd been known as a really crappy athlete and a mediocre dancer. Casey, his roommate freshman year, liked to call him the Living Anti-Cliché. What he'd been good at was playing poker. He could keep numbers and visual stuff in his head. He might've become a banker, easily—Casey told him—if he'd had a completely different character. These days Marcus had to stop himself from playing games of solitaire over and over on his cell phone. Solitaire—talk about clichés of the lonely lover. No! He wasn't doing that.

At breakfast, Casey said, "Wanna swim today? Swimming will do you good."

Casey drove too sloppily on the curving mountain roads, and then they all had to clamber through brambles and probably poison ivy, but Marcus stopped being grouchy once they got down to the glinting creek. The place had a dappled stillness, even with clusters of shrieking, splashing kids. It was fringed with ferns and dark tiers of rocks, with an elegant little waterfall you could stand under. The water was deeper in one spot than Marcus had thought, and he entered the shocking coolness of it, paddling and kicking and darting in circles.

He was fine for the rest of the day too. Anyone seeing

him, at the pizza place for lunch, at the farm stand buying
corn, on the back road taking a little stroll with Casey and
Carol, whom he loved, would have thought he was fine, and
would not have guessed for a minute that part of him was
wallowing in despair and was only waiting to be alone and
get back to his book.

The book, which he managed to open before supper, had the
narrator (someone named Norman F. Remsen, who had never
become famous) going to consult his dear friend Dorothy
Day. (Marcus knew who *she* was, though she was apparently
unfamous at this point, way before she started the *Catholic
Worker*.) The narrator was sure Dorothy would never blab
anything she happened to know about who Betsy was sleeping with, but he hoped she might slip. Dorothy was having a
hard winter, living alone with her kid, who was almost three,
in dark, narrow "housekeeping rooms" on Fourteenth Street.
She gave the narrator a cup of tea. "After I dutifully admired
her rather serious little daughter, I said, 'Betsy meant to come
with me but couldn't. She's come before, yes?' Betsy had told
me this more than once—I didn't believe her—and I was
driven to see if Dorothy would feel she had to cover for her.
Women are always loyal to each other. But Dorothy was not
one to lie. In fact, she failed to reply—she bustled about
fetching crackers and jam for us, and then little Tamar had to
be helped with her snack." The episode ended with Norman
behaving churlishly—condescending to Dorothy and complaining viciously about the politics of his friends. But when
he went home, he couldn't help thinking that Dorothy had

acted on principle, leaving her baby's father for her beliefs, and that she had avoided making a fool of herself for love, as he was so busy doing.

At dinner that night, Marcus tried to tell his friends about the book. "He's a politico whose wife is running around on him. This part is like a mystery where you guess who the dickhead is."

"Memoirs are so weird," Carol said. "He probably made it all up."

"He's howling about his heartbreak right now," Marcus said. "On the page it's touching but in real life he was probably unbearable to be around."

"People can be unbearable if they want," Carol said.

"A little moaning is fine," Casey said.

"I think he's going to punch his wife," Marcus said. "I can't wait. Is that totally wrong of me?"

"Yes," Carol said.

Marcus had been with Nico for five years, which was really not such a long time. Probably Nico had always wanted someone more glamorous. Their Brooklyn apartment—half a brownstone in Cobble Hill, with a little yard in the back—was now Nico's, and Marcus was in a bare, silly studio in downtown Brooklyn. When would he stop hating his life? Sometimes he caught sight of himself in the mirror and he thought, *That sucker looks so pathetic*. The wincing eyes, the clamped jaw. And that was his public face. In the dark he probably looked like ashes and dirt. When he woke up out of his sleep, he was a naked bag of bones too familiar to himself. He'd never believed it would last forever with Nico, but the thought of that only compounded his suffering.

It was not, of course, the only suffering in the world. Marcus knew what the world was. Every day he read the news, with its war atrocities and massacres of civilians, rape camps, drug murders, nuclear disaster. Year after year he filed papers for clients who lived with rats, leaking sewage, lead paint, guns in the elevator. He'd spent time in India, seen the streets of Mumbai. He wasn't a sap.

Marcus did not rush off to read after dinner. He did the dishes, he heard Carol tell a funny story about deer getting into their garden. He and Casey played a ridiculous game of Frisbee in the dark, running and jumping for the phantom disk, and horsing around as if they weren't both in their late thirties already. He was properly tired when he went back to his room. He'd had a full day and was ready to be fast asleep in his sweet, musty garret on the top floor. He didn't think he would read tonight, but he did.

The author was having a peevish argument with his wife Betsy. She made fun of his household economies—he saved string from packages, he tried to get her to darn socks and turn his collars, to cook variety meats. "Cheapness is a moral virtue to you," she said.

"It is," he said. "That's how we manage to live without selling ourselves."

Betsy laughed at him. He had never seen her do this

before—her face was full of merry scorn—and he began shouting at her. "I have mercifully forgotten the words I shouted, but I know that I had to keep myself from striking her. I was a young man with a good opinion of myself; every thought I had was against violence and domination, and it was a dreadful shock to find myself thus. I had my hand in the air, ready to strike at her face, and Betsy screeched in fear."

Marcus sort of liked the smart-ass Betsy, whose revolutionary spirit had probably been a matter of disposition more than politics. She was too much for the author, that was clear.

The poor husband's apologies put an end to the fight, but Marcus could tell more was in store. Early in the morning, just past dawn, he read the rest. Terrified of losing Betsy, the repentant husband turned to the desperate strategy of buying her a string of glass beads—in red, her favorite color—to make amends. In hock to all his friends, he could only think to ask Joe's wife, Vera, for a loan, though he had never stooped to borrowing from a woman before. Vera was apparently an eager, mousy, vain person, easily persuaded. Betsy was delighted with the necklace and thanked him afterward with hugs and kisses and other things not quite mentioned on the page.

Just as the author was sure his suspicions of her had been unfair, Betsy spilled the beans. She was leaving him for the man who ran the speakeasy. What man? Marcus had guessed nothing and was angry at the writer for failing to give clues. Not playing fair with the reader.

"You might have thought this woman joining herself with an ordinary barkeep did not have an idea in her head. Betsy had plenty of ideas, but she chose to abandon them. She wanted to live out of a lesser part of herself, whereas I was trying for better. I seemed a prig to her when I said it, but that is the flame I have lived by."

He did sound priggish there, but Marcus was basically with him.

The humiliated author wanted to get out of town so badly he managed, by scrimping and selling off whatever he owned and probably more borrowing, to get hold finally of a cheap boat ticket to Europe. "In Paris I was able to connect with fellow radicals. But I found this final separation from Betsy very painful—I was often in sorry shape those first months and spoke of little else but my loss. I might have thought Paris, City of Love, would lend an ear, but people showed great impatience and lack of interest. Who was I to them? My French was terrible, their English was often not very good. They had their own concerns. A number of them ventured forth to help comrades menaced by brutal police in Fascist Italy, and not all those who crossed the border returned. I understood that my own wounded heart was a weak topic in light of this bloodshed.

"My sojourn here has had its interruptions and hardships, but Paris has given me sustenance and joy, in the form of my dear wife and companion, Josette LeBlanc, and it blesses me now in my current satisfying life."

This was not the book's ending—there was another chapter, about old Villagers he ran into on the Boul' Mich'—this was just a brief, sunny summary, a golden flash-forward. He couldn't resist a surge of sentiment. And if that bumbling young putz could find lasting happiness, anyone could.

• • •

Nico would've liked such a book. Marcus had in fact picked it up half imitating Nico—Nico was a great collector of vintage postcards, moldy collections of obscure essays, photos of union picnics. The tinted and dusty surfaces of submerged characters called to him. Marcus wondered how many years he would spend acting out Nico's old habits, just to keep him around.

And what did the author ever think he was doing, with his champagne cocktails and necklaces for Betsy? What kind of anarchist thinks money buys love? But a lover tries anything, that's how it is. Gandhi's alleged lover, Hermann Kallenbach, had donated all the land for a communal farm and training center that Gandhi set up in South Africa. Not that anyone thought Gandhi had given his body for cash.

In India, not so long ago, Marcus had been like Kallenbach—he'd tried to court someone with money. In Mumbai, of all places. He hadn't even meant to go to India, but he'd been having trouble at work (lost a case it hurt to lose) and wanted to go somewhere far, far away. Someone must've told him India was wonderful. Which it was, in many ways. Fabulous elaborate temples, Bollywood billboards, women in glorious saris, flowers like Technicolor props. His modest hotel was right on the road that ran along the sea, with lovely breakfasts on the porch, and at first he thought, *It's not bad here at all*. He wrote postcards showing the colonial Gothic hulk of the Victoria Terminus and he raved about the sunset at Chowpatty Beach. Nothing too terrible on the streets, not for a New Yorker. It took another day for him to meet what was waiting—the beggar with no legs pushing himself on a board with wheels, the tiny begging children leading tinier children, the skeletal old woman with hands like claws holding an infant up to a car window to beg. An Indian at his hotel tried to tell him that the beggars worked for gangsters and staged their plight. "Not getting fat at it, are they?" Marcus said.

He heard himself tell all sorts of fellow travelers that he couldn't understand why there hadn't been a revolt of the masses in India. Indians he met offered explanations—the caste system, fatalism, colonialism, corrupt leaders—or laughed at the silliness of the question. Marcus came to think that the question was a religious one: *What the fuck is the matter with people? This isn't going away, is it?*

And for all his burning thought, Marcus was in collusion. He gave coins now and then, but mostly not. He'd become someone who was afraid of poor people. Him! It shocked him each time someone took hold of his arm or followed him for blocks. A perfectly nice Australian woman he often spoke to at breakfast said, "You can't save everyone." Marcus thought that was so not the point.

On a particularly hot day, Marcus took himself to a Gandhi museum (his book said there was one in almost every city), and it was the first consoling thing he'd done. The museum was just somebody's house where Gandhi had stayed on visits to Bombay, crammed now with exhibits, plus a plaque where he used to pitch a tent on the terrace. Marcus listened to Gandhi's voice in Hindi, telling people to purify themselves while he fasted for Hindu-Muslim unity, a recording made two weeks before he was shot. *When I leave this museum,*

Marcus thought, *I'll give most of the rupees in my wallet to the first beggar I meet.*

Another tourist, looking at a copy of Gandhi's passport, said, "They've forgotten him, even if he's a hero. Nobody wants to do what he did."

"I know," Marcus said. "How did that happen?" The man was American, about Marcus's age. Not bad-looking, with a very short haircut and sly, half-squinting eyes.

"He was a fluke," the man said. "One of a kind."

"History doesn't have flukes," Marcus said. Not that he believed that—maybe history had nothing but flukes—but he seemed to want to keep talking to the guy. "And he wasn't alone, it wasn't just him."

"He started it," the man said. "The British just thought he was a crazy fool."

They moved past oddly pretty dioramas in black frames, with finely molded mini-figures depicting the life of Gandhi, from the child stealing a piece of gold and repenting to his father, to the body in a sandalwood pyre (Lead me from the Unreal to the Real), in twenty-eight tableaux, and when the guy looked ready to leave, Marcus said, "Want to join me for coffee? Or something cold?"

So no lucky pauper of Mumbai was blessed with the contents of Marcus's wallet as he left the museum. He could not have said where he passed the first beggar or whether none went by at all, since he was caught up in conversation and gave no attention to anything else. His new friend was a doctor, it turned out, from D.C. but moving soon to New York, which was certainly a very good piece of news. The man was an oncologist, which Marcus thought could not be a happy profession, and yet he seemed far less depressed than anyone Marcus knew, and they had the happiest, most sociable of afternoons. They drank exquisitely cold Kingfisher beers and sat for a long time in an air-conditioned café talking about how good it was to be away from work, although they loved their work. "I could've picked something easier, but I didn't," the man said. He was going back home the next morning.

And was there anything wrong with Marcus insisting on taking him out for a glorious, expensive dinner? Nothing wrong at all, except that Marcus was not even remotely a man who liked to go on such outings—but he had seen, by then, the need to be (for this person) someone with a bolder style and a sexy streak of extravagance, someone who did not take *every*thing seriously. Who wants to sleep with a hangdog?

And the evening had gone very well. After the Cochin oysters with cucumber and lime granita, and the pork chop pistou with Kashmiri apple curry, and the coconut sago crepes, in a restaurant with a reflecting pool with marigolds floating in it, Marcus had gone back to the man's hotel room and they had had a night of tremendous mutual understanding. How subtle, how intelligent the man's senses were. Just after dawn Marcus rose from bed with him and said, before he took himself out the door, "This was very lucky for me."

And Nico, for it was Nico, said, "Don't think we can't continue on another continent."

Five days later, when Marcus himself was at the airport, he remembered that he hadn't ever gotten around to giving the next destitute street person he met most of the cash in his wallet. He had only a clump of leftover rupees he was about to try to change—maybe thirteen dollars in American money—and he left these in the tip saucer of the men's room attendant at the airport. Much more than the man would expect to get from anybody, and Marcus felt quite good about it, at first.

In his law firm Marcus had the reputation of being testy and driven but good at what he did. When he came back from India, a secretary said, "I hope you had time to chill," and Marcus decided it was time to stop being a pain to everyone, and (he'd thought about it before) he got himself into this semi-Catholic the-Desert-Fathers-started-it Christian meditation, which it turned out he liked. Nico, whom he was seeing long-distance at the time, thought it was a little weird (it wasn't regular prayer? what was it? no drugs involved? why not?) but Marcus didn't mind being teased. Not by Nico, not then.

Marcus could remember those long train rides to Washington on Friday nights, when Nico lived there. The darkened railroad car was full of people sleeping, and Marcus had loved the stillness, the mystery of the train moving through the night, and his own anticipation, his sleepless joy.

Six months later, when they were moving together into a very nice house in Brooklyn, Nico was driven crazy—stark raving out of his mind with vexation—from lying contractors, bad wiring, plumbers who never showed up. Marcus said, "It'll get done, houses always get done."

Nico said, "It's the meditation, isn't it? It's done you good. Listen to you."

"What?" Marcus said. "Oh, no, it isn't that. It's India." What he meant was that his instinct to complain had been damaged by the trip, his perspective altered by the memory of encampments at night in the streets, kids curled up together on the pavement. Comparatively speaking, he and Nico had no fucking problems.

Did that mean he was calmer? Maybe. Nico said there were people, after trips like that, who clung even harder to what they had, for fear of losing it and becoming God-knew-what. Why wasn't Marcus afraid?

"The house isn't everything," Marcus said.

"Don't annoy me," Nico said.

When he and Nico were first together they'd had an argument about religion. Not a serious argument. Marcus believed in Something Divine (he'd been raised Catholic) and Nico thought it was all horseshit. Marcus also said Jesus was a Communist, which Nico was willing to go with. Those were the more crucial sympathies, their views on justice and profits. They couldn't have stayed together for more than an hour otherwise.

Around Zuccotti Park, when Marcus had marched one night with the Occupy Wall Streeters, there was a kid dressed as Jesus (robe, beard, halo) with the sign YOU HAVE NOTHING TO LOSE BUT YOUR CHAINS. Marcus himself carried a poster that said IF A LAWYER MARCHES, YOU KNOW IT'S SERIOUS. Marcus thought now that the anarchists in *Village Days and Nights* would've been very cheered to see all of it.

Someone had taken a nice photo of Marcus walking with

his sign. He looked skinny but determined, chin up, sunglasses on. Did he look handsome? Did Nico still have his copy?

On Sunday morning, in Casey and Carol's kitchen, they all sat around reading newspapers on their laptops and iPads and they didn't speak much. They had known one another a very long time. Casey and Marcus had stayed friends all through college, and when Carol came on the scene, a few years later, Marcus had been really very pleased with Casey's choice. Nico had found them a dowdy but endearing couple. (Could've been worse.)

Nico had his snobberies. He was the world's best-dressed oncologist, with his pristine striped shirt and handsome tie peeping out from his lab coat. Did it make his patients (none of them in good shape) think he knew what he was doing? Once, when Marcus cut his finger in the kitchen, Nico had bandaged it, and Marcus had found himself oddly moved by the sureness of his hands.

"No one is predicting improvement in the job figures," Carol said, looking up from a Sunday Review page. "They've stopped pretending to be upbeat."

"In that memoir I was reading," Marcus said, "the guy hardly mentions the Depression. Doesn't bother with it. Can you believe that?"

"He got obsessed with his own story," Carol said. "People do."

"Anarchists aren't supposed to be surprised if world markets self-destruct," Casey said.

"Well, he didn't own much," Marcus said.

"Not like us," Carol said.

Marcus was Googling Norman F. Remsen, who had no listing except one for the book, used, for $3.45, on Amazon. Marcus decided to look up Gandhi's sex life, while he was at it. The writer of the most recent biography was quoted as saying he personally thought Gandhi and Kallenbach had been celibate soul mates, attracted maybe but loyal to their vows of continence.

Marcus noticed he was thinking of swiping *Village Days and Nights* from the house (Casey wouldn't care) and taking it to Nico. He'd just call Nico up and say, *I found this thing, wait till you see.* Oh! He wanted to give Nico a present! Was that not the stupidest thing in the world?

Carol, who was now scarfing down a bowl of cereal, said, "You look better today."

"It's the mountain air," Marcus said. "The stars at night."

He had not even really noticed the stars at night, but he liked the idea of them. Had they been out when he and Casey were playing midnight Frisbee? He couldn't remember.

"Yes, I can see you're awed by it all," Casey said.

"Awe is so overrated."

The real lover of nature had been Nico, unlikely though that seemed to everyone. He used to drag Marcus on walks through Prospect Park at excessively early hours of the morning to check out the new bird arrivals with his binoculars. In spring there were warblers of many obscure kinds. Marcus could never get over the sight of the ever-chic Nico peering through those clunky lenses into the sycamores and oaks and the leaf-strewn dirt. How intent he was then, how solemn with interest. One bleak day in late February, when Marcus had refused to get up and go all the way to Central Park for new sightings, Nico came home thrilled about seeing the first spring migrant, the American woodcock. There were many jokes about the name (who else would be hanging out in the Ramble?) and photos on his cell phone of some splotchy brownish bird with a long beak doing a turkey trot. "I'm a happy man," Nico said, and he was, glowing and grinning. It made Marcus think about what happiness was. For how long had Nico seen that bird—maybe ninety seconds? Of course, now it was enshrined forever in the memory of his iPhone, kept like any bit of joy in the brain. Not the real bird, but something.

Nico, who was nothing if not generous, had bought Marcus his own pair of binoculars, an allegedly very good kind. Marcus had taken them with him when he packed all his stuff, but what did he need them for? They seemed to be especially painful to look at because he had never used them. He really did not want to dwell on any of this. They were in a cardboard box pushed to the back of a closet, and there was no need to picture them.

He'd thought he was better. Why wasn't he better? Why couldn't he leave himself alone? He was worse than the memoir writer annoying everyone in Paris. What was so irresistible about freshening his own mortal agony every fucking second?

In these first months of this stage of his life, he had no choice but to marshal what powers he had to keep himself from slipping full-time into being a sorry specimen. A person who meditated was supposed to have some sense that the mind could occasionally control itself. In India, he'd heard about holy men standing on one leg for years, lying on beds of cacti, going naked in Himalayan snow. Marcus hadn't seen any of that and was just as glad he hadn't. But sadhus could do those things and more. No wonder Westerners hardly understood Gandhi.

What he remembered best about India was sitting in the café in Mumbai with Nico. This was before it was entirely clear something was about to happen, when a shimmering prospect just hovered in the air. Nico had laughed at an ordinary crack Marcus made about his job—he said Housing Court had a sitcom in every chamber—and Marcus saw the gathered lines around Nico's eyes, the flash in them, the beam of his teeth. These commonplace signs of another human spirit embodied in a highly specific physical form seemed just so, so remarkable to him. Marcus found himself telling his only good landlord joke (what do landlords use for birth control? their personalities)—Marcus never told jokes!—and they were very jolly together, the two of them.

Earlier in the day—only hours before—Marcus had not been in a good mood at all. He was burdened by what he saw in India, by the case he'd lost at home (rent strikers evicted by well-connected sleazeball), and by existential exhaustion. When he turned the corner to walk toward the Gandhi museum, he was thinking, *It's too hot, what an insane country, I have to get out of here,* and *Where else is anything ever better?*

At least it was cool inside, all polished wood and things behind glass. How weird Gandhi looked in some of those pictures, wizened, ghost-eyed, half naked. The Desert Fathers, fasting in their cells, had nothing on him. There was a photo from the Salt March, Gandhi on the road with a stream of white-clad followers behind him, ready to harvest salt illegally from the sea. The freaked-out British ended up putting sixty thousand people in prison when salt defiance spread over India. Mounted cops (Marcus read) charged one group and they saved themselves by lying flat on the ground. Whose idea was that? What Marcus wanted to know was: How long had those people trained themselves to do such a thing? When had they decided to be better than they ever thought they wanted to be?

Marcus had gotten lost twice before finding the museum, people were hard to understand and gave bad directions. Why should he find himself consoled there? But he did. He remembered very clearly now that he did.

Going Too Far

When I was a boy, my father was always leaving us and coming back and disappearing again. When he was home, he managed to gamble away all the cash in the house, no matter where my mother hid it. Florida had a lot of temptations for a guy who couldn't resist a bet. He did have moments of being jolly, of acting as if he got a big kick out of everything about us. He bought me a bike when he was flush, a Raleigh English racer, black with silver, very cool—"Here, Gerard, knock yourself out," he said—and he sold it three months later. My mother threw him out for good when I started junior high. I wanted him back and I didn't.

My mother was glad to have a steady job and she was very loyal to the hotel where she worked. People were, in those days. She was the head bookkeeper. "Ask Millie in the office" was such an all-purpose solution that Betsy, one of the hotel's owners, gave my mom a pillow with this embroidered on it, as a tribute. And my mother loved that pillow. When I visited her at work, I was fed treats from the hotel kitchen—glistening hamburgers, hot caramel sundaes—but was not allowed to swim in the pool. Luís, the desk manager, played dominoes with me and let me show him my baseball cards.

When I was in ninth grade, my mother said, "Will you listen for a second? Stop eating and listen. I might get fired." A sizable wad of cash was missing from the till. Betsy said she'd always trusted my mother in spite of her having an unsavory family situation. Everyone knew about my father. Betsy suggested that the thief, whoever it was, would do well to just put the money back before the police were alerted. They questioned Luís too. "They think we're up to funny business together," my mother said. "It's ridiculous but I'm not laughing."

"Luís is an old guy!" I said.

My mother, who was not that old for a mother, was weepy instead of loud and indignant. I did wonder if my father had managed to sneak into the hotel office without her knowing. Maybe her agony was in thinking this too. At the end of the week they left her alone but they fired Luís.

"Is he going to jail?" I said.

"Luís didn't do anything!" she said. "You know Luís!"

Mr. Elegant Old Coot, Mr. Silver Fox, with his mustache and his deep, deep voice. He'd worked at that goddamn hotel longer than my mother.

"And nobody cares," my mother said. "The union doesn't care."

• • •

The rank and stinking wrongness of it made me want to push the entire hotel into the sea. At the time, I saw the corruptions of the world as things to be trashed and slashed and ridiculed, I saw them from what might be called a criminal angle. Later I had other theories. I got my friend Dick, who was old enough to drive a car, to take me past the hotel at midnight, and we lit cherry bombs (what thrills of utter panic) and threw them—fast, fast—toward the empty lawn, where they landed in the bushes and exploded with great cracking booms, just as we peeled out of there. We could hear people shouting from the veranda above.

From the traffic light down the road, we looked back and saw flames in the bushes, which some poor sucker in a hotel uniform was going to have to put out. Dick, a perfectly nice guy, was slamming his hand on the steering wheel in savage glee. I whooped too, I did.

It scared the hell out of the guests—we knew this right away and heard for sure later. Let them leave, yes. Let this be the hotel's worst October ever. The hotel told everyone it was pre-Halloween mischief, local kids gone wild. We lived in West Palm and weren't even that local. My mother thought it was Luís's kids, and maybe lots of people did.

A week later we all found out that the owners' sleazy son was the one who'd made off with the missing money. And he was in some foreign country where no one could get to him. Luís was rehired, with apologies. But without his missing week's pay. "They can never make it up to him," my mother said. "Look at him. Look what they did to him."

She was talking also about herself, the end to her cozy infatuation with her daily toil. She came home tired and sour. I was out of the house as much as I could be, pursuing my new hobbies. The elation of the cherry bomb attack was my gateway drug to further excitements of vandalism. We dumped human turds on somebody's lovely private beach, we broke into my junior high and spray-painted *Fuck Shit Cum* all over the auditorium. It was pretty spectacular. Dick and I took a vow of silence, which we actually kept, and that was probably the only reason we weren't caught.

If you're testing your nerve, you need to keep going further. The next year, Dick's friend Alan showed us how to break into and hot-wire a big fat white Pontiac parked outside the movie theater and we took it for a proverbial joy-ride, blasting the radio down the highway to Boca Raton and back. What I felt on that ride was a soaring belief, a white light of certainty, that we were really awake and most people were slaves and were asleep.

We did brag about that one. I was only fifteen, younger than the others, and I didn't have girls to impress, but none of us kept our mouths shut. Which brought girls to me, in fact. Nicolette from my American History class started to hang around after the bell. She was okay, a bratty, complicated girl with a great rear end. Her friend Susan liked me too.

Once I was fooling around with girls, I had enough adventures at night to draw me away from mayhem with Dick and Alan. Somewhat. At the end of the summer the three of us set a magnificent bonfire on the beach and it took out a piece of somebody's wharf. Well, that was fun to watch. I continued to do surprisingly well in school, much to my mother's relief. This was partly because school was contemptibly easy, and partly because I still liked (as I always had) the privacy of reading. My mother said, "If you just remember you're not the idiot you pretend to be, you'll be fine. More than fine." She said this fondly, patting my shoulder. She even laughed when I made an idiot face and pretended to drool. This may have been around the time she started having an affair with Luís, which made her quite happy for a while.

Luís was never going to divorce his wife. My mother (who got more confidential about the whole thing as time went on) was sure this was because he was Catholic, though it was clear to me he had plenty of other reasons. We were Jewish. (Even my father was.) They never sent me to Hebrew school or bothered with much of it, but now my mother proudly invoked Jewish tolerance of divorce. "What does the Pope know about marriage?" she said. "And birth control! Don't get me started."

What if you really thought there was a God (I didn't) and you thought His rules were wrong? My mother said you could join another religion. "Let's convert Luís to Muhammadism, and then he can have a lot of wives," I said.

"Very funny," my mother said. "Use your brain for something useful."

Her thing with Luís went on for years. I went off to college (to Minnesota, where the winters were too cold and I had a scholarship) and I came home on vacations to find my mother all in knots about some new insult or frustration in her underground romance. My friends said, "At least she's getting some," which was a crude version of what I sort of thought. I did know, as well then as ever, what splendor my mother found in whatever she had with Luís, but I was too young to see why it would make her put up with all the other crap.

In college I myself had a lot of hot and fleeting romances. We enjoyed our drugs, in those days, and the mix of marijuana and sex was considered a personal revelation, a sacred message we each happened to decode. And I could never keep from talking about whether the mind was all chemicals and what that proved, conversely, about matter's connection to spirit. I liked those airy arguments. In my head they were linked to the overwhelming evidence that the mundane world around me ran on hypocritical horseshit. Everything was in collusion to hide the truth, and my friend Dick from high school was drafted and sent to Da Nang on the word of government liars. I showed the kids from SDS how to throw a burning effigy of President Nixon on to the college lawn so that it torched some famous oak tree, which was kind of great to see. I engineered a small exploding rocket in front of the ROTC the next year, but I stopped there.

I never got into enough public trouble to risk my scholarship. I had to be careful. And by the time I graduated, I'd found my own sources for buying dope in quantity and was supplying a good part of the campus, at a very fair price.

I liked my day as a local big shot, but I knew from the years with my father the dangers of overestimating your own luck. My ambition in life was to go far but stay safe. Once I was out of school, I moved around, to Chicago and then to northern California, trying to get a handle on what I could do and not do. In San Francisco I had a girlfriend who was getting her master's in art history and working as a stripper. What a strange and fabulous creature she was. While she slept beside me, after her night of professional display and private love, I rose from bed each morning, in a great act of will, and went to my steady gig at the state unemployment benefits office. They had me (what a joke) interviewing people about their job searches and approving their continuing payments. I was very lenient.

That summer, my mother made one too many demands on Luís and he decided at long last, with much apology and probably genuine sorrow, to put an end to their romance, right at the time Sandie, my stripper girlfriend, ran off with the bass player in the club band. My mother and I had odd, dry, sad little conversations about how things would get better eventually. We were both ripped to shreds. My mother took refuge in Miller Lite and TV and weekly bridge games. I went to Zen meditation groups and Sufi concerts and Sikh Dharma talks. There was a lot of that around and some of it helped me, with its elaborated reiterations that there was more to care about than any Sandie.

One night I was sitting on the floor in the basement of a bookstore, watching Sufi dervishes twirl around and around, their white robes flaring like sails, their arms outstretched. They were mostly just plain old Americans like me, but they wore high brownish caps someone told me were tombs for the ego, and they pivoted on soft boots, circling in place, while the music was plucked and blown and beaten by musicians. All of this was designed to take them on an inner journey from which they emerged no longer caring about petty crap. I knew that much, which was not a lot. I sank into it enough to say afterward, "Hey! Amazing!" to the guy next to me, who was going out for a beer with some other people, and that was how I met Adinah.

There were maybe ten of us, filing into a smoky bar, and we got reshuffled so that this small-faced woman with fuzzy tendrils of pale hair was looking up at me. "I'm still dazed from watching those guys," I said.

"Is this your first time?" she said. Probably this wasn't the pickup line it sounded like.

"I plan to come back," I said.

But it turned out her allegiance was to another Sufi group that had music but none of this whirling. "If you're repeating God's name inside, you don't need to have this *performance*," she said.

"Don't be a bigot," one of the women said. "I hate it when you get like that, Adinah. You're so sectarian."

"They have to focus when they twirl," some guy said. "If they have worldly thoughts while they're doing it, they get dizzy and collapse."

"Adinah just likes her own fucking group," another woman said.

"This is like the Middle Ages!" I said. "I'm in the middle of warring religious factions."

I said this out of feeling uncomfortable, but to my surprise Adinah thought it was funny. "We are such assholes," she said cheerfully.

I had ordered a big pile of gooey nachos for the table, and she turned out to be one of those skinny girls who ate very slowly and neatly. She worked, she said, as a waitress in a vegetarian restaurant. "I bet they're not big tippers, those veges," I said.

"You guessed right," she said. She didn't look like someone who could have worked in a bar for real cash. Too skittish and big-eyed.

"What's your favorite vegetable?" somebody at the table asked.

Everybody nominated a favorite sexy shape—the women picked giant zucchini, the guys went fruitarian and chose melons, with pantomimes to suggest the breastiness of them. Adinah just laughed, with her hand over her mouth.

This same shyness kept her from going home with me at the end of the night, although I thought she liked me. I gave her and about five other people a squished ride home in my old VW Beetle and I made sure to drop her off last. "To be continued," she said, looking straight at me when I took her hand, but she got herself out of the car fast. I could see she was someone I had to go slow with.

So how could I be with someone like her after being with Sandie? I had no trouble, even in the early stages, intuiting the intensity of Adinah, the nuclear heat under the wispy flutter. She was quiet but she was never really mild. The soft pitch of her voice had the cadence of a strong will. And there was a fearless streak, as yet just a streak. Of the two of us, I was the more moderate, the more deliberating.

I went with her to classes given by her own particular Sufi group—their founder was from India, not Turkey—and

I didn't just do this in hopes of getting laid. I had other hopes too, of getting out of myself, of slipping into something larger than where I'd always lived. It was harder than I'd thought. There I was, apologizing to God for my separation from Him, when I didn't exactly believe in God. But I had glimpses of another realm I might rise to later, if I could get more adept. It was interesting. I was very interested in the progress of my fate.

At the Sufi classes we moved our heads, swaying them to the right and then nodding down, saying no to petty bullshit and yes to God, over and over, while someone played an amazing giant lute called a tamboura and sang chants. He was still called Allah in the chants, and why not? We breathed in and out, we opened our hearts to God's presence. I drove Adinah home across the Bay after the classes, and she'd sit talking to me in the car before she went in.

By the time Adinah and I became lovers, we had, in some way, beaten each other down. I had shaken off some of my boy-bluster, and she had grown more pliant, more hopeful. She muttered a prayer before she got into bed with me! I didn't know what it was (she made it up), and it spooked me before my body decided, on its own, to be sublimely flattered. How naked she was, all of a sudden, turning to me, how familiarly female. I was sure I could carry us where we wanted to go. She muttered my name, nothing new in that, but it was a new and ardent form of Adinah.

She hadn't had more than four lovers before me, but she knew herself better than some women do. She had great freedom in her, great ease, and then later, when we woke from our shared sleep and I watched her dress, putting on her dainty cotton underwear, a certain shyness came back and she was gawky as a chicken. *Look at her*, I thought. I could not have been more susceptible.

It was only the week before we first slept together that I'd heard she was from a family of Orthodox Jews. All her schooling had been in Jewish girls' schools until college—and then she'd gone to Berkeley, of all places. Berserkly, as we liked to call it. She hadn't been home to New York in three years. Her parents' phone calls were still full of anger and pleading. "You're all mixed up," they said, sometimes with tears.

"They won't give up," she said. "They can't."

No, they didn't know she went to any Sufi group. They already thought she was wild and promiscuous (ha) and addled with drugs. The Sufi group we followed was no longer attached to Islam anyway and proclaimed itself universal and tolerant. This explanation, Adinah said, would have gone nowhere with her parents. They would have shrieked to hear it. I wasn't used to parents like that—I thought they were part of a world that had faded long since and was surprised they were so powerful to Adinah.

I told my own mother about Adinah and my mother said, "So she's on her own now. They won't make it easy." My mother knew more about it than I did. After Adinah had sort of moved in with me, my mother liked to chat with her. Whether California had better weather than Florida, what Adinah made us for dinner. "Your mother has a nice personality," Adinah said.

My own philosophical conflict with Adinah had to do with her being a vegetarian. She said what I ate was my own business, but the smell of meat made her nauseous. I didn't really mind eating eggplant parmigiana or even soybean loaf for dinner, but I was naturally wary of being pussy-whipped. So we worked out some elaborate treaty, whereby I could store cooked meat (like bologna or liverwurst) in one corner of the fridge if I didn't eat it in front of her. Like most compromises, this made neither of us happy, but we bragged of it so much to friends we began to believe we were peacemakers in love. Which was not untrue.

Adinah had been sharing a cottage in Berkeley with a swarm of people, so she didn't have tons of belongings when she moved in with me. All the same, after the first blast of mutual joy, we were kind of crowded in my small space, never out of each other's sight. So I got together some bucks left over from a minor marijuana deal Sandie had helped me with the year before, and I ponied it up for realtor's fees and security, and I moved Adinah and me into a bigger apartment, on a hilly block in Noe Valley. The rent wasn't a bargain, but I did have a salary.

I loved that apartment. It had a big bay window in the living room and great old woodwork and rooms full of nooks and crannies, very San Francisco. Adinah was touched that I'd done this for both of us, and, of course, I was touched too. I rented a sander and got the floors scraped to the nub, and then we practically asphyxiated ourselves swabbing polyurethane over them. I was the director of all of this, and she was my household. "I hate this job," she said, happily. She wanted to name the apartment, the way people name a boat or sometimes a car, but I thought that was going too far.

Nonetheless she named it. We lived in "Heaven's Door," after the Dylan tune, knock, knock, knockin' on. I pointed out that in the song the guy was dying, but she didn't care. "It's about the death of the lesser self," she said. Well, I liked the song. "Want to go back to the Door?" she'd ask, when we'd been out at a party long enough. Even I started saying, "The Door is so big it keeps eating my socks."

We had a mini-view of the eastern sky out the kitchen window, and we were always congratulating ourselves on this peek of cloudy white over the neighboring roofs. One unusually clear night we spotted the sliver of the new moon, and Adinah said, "Oh, there are prayers for that." She meant Jewish prayers. For the moon? I'd never heard of such a thing. So were the Orthodox into astrology too? "*No,*" she said. "And it sounds better than it was." I could hardly imagine the world she came from, with its rituals daily, weekly, monthly. "I like this moon better," she said. "Our moon."

Adinah's parents didn't have our phone number, but sometimes they called her at the restaurant where she worked. One night she told me, "You know what they called to tell me one more time? I was helping the enemies of the Jews by denying who I was, and I was only kidding myself if I thought otherwise. They worked their way into it at the end of the conversation."

"They waited that long?"

She let out a little mirthless laugh. I put my arms around her for comfort. It was terrible to me that parents, of all people, could be this cruel to someone as gentle as Adinah. Who never said a really mean word about anyone. Who covered her eyes at any bloodshed on TV. I was glad she had me, at least, her personal fortress to lean on. "They'll get used to your being this way," I said.

"No, they won't," she said.

• • •

I'd known waitresses who made good livings, but Adinah, who worked lunches, was not one of them. The rent came from me, which I didn't mind. We were managing fine, until my rust bucket of a Volkswagen broke down on the way home from work and I had to pay to get it towed and then it needed a new transmission. I was sure that when the end of the month came I would somehow have enough cash on hand for the rent, and I told Adinah it was *no problemo*, but then as the days went by I saw we had a bit of an emergency on our hands. What surprised me in all this was Adinah.

"You have to do something," she said. "You better do something."

"I know that," I said.

"We can't lose the apartment. Why did we ever get it if you're just going to lose it?"

"I'm doing my best, baby," I said.

"I think I believe you," she said.

The last thing I expected from my doe-eyed girl was to be *pressured*. Was she venal at heart, looking for what my mother would call a lunch ticket? This made me remember she'd been eating almost nothing, to help save us, and I understood she was simply scared stiff. But I was still pissed at her.

On the other hand, I knew what I had to do. I called my friend Art, who got in touch with a guy named Spud, and with my last paycheck I bought as much as I could of this high-quality Michoacán grass he had just gotten in. And I wasn't short on customers—from my office, from Adinah's restaurant, from our Sufi group. I got us through the crisis just fine, and the two of us had laughing fits watching TV commercials stoned when we were home celebrating the rent payment. The Frito Bandito was pretty funny. Adinah, with her head on my shoulder, snorted and hooted into my neck.

But I didn't like it. You had to be a certain way when you were buying in bulk. You had to drive to some creepy bungalow in the middle of nowhere, walk in quiet as a cowboy, sampling a joint and muttering *Nice, very nice,* rubbing the dope between your fingers, making a few worldly wisecracks, shaking the hand of some joker with guns in the house, watching your back every second. Then ride the highway with your radioactive cargo. You were talking yourself into thinking you were one sly dude with balls of steel, you were no one to mess with. This is why people get hurt if they surprise a robber. He's busy *being* a robber. It's why they have to rev up soldiers to be soldiers.

I kept those kilos of dope wrapped in a quilt in a closet in the tiny room Adinah used for meditation. I didn't want a single one of our many customers to see how much I had. We hadn't lived in the building that long, and a grandmotherly type across the hall said, "You get a lot of company these days."

"The door is always open to our friends," I said.

"Is that a fact?" she said.

So I had to worry about her too. Who knew who she was? All she had to do was make a phone call. I took it out on Adinah, who had wheedled me into this. "Are you comfortable on that sofa?" I said. "Maybe you want us to get a more expensive sofa."

"Me?" she said. "Not me. I like the opposite. I left the land of white satin sofas and plastic slipcovers. That's why I'm here."

"You're still a princess," I said.

"Of what?"

"Like the princess and the pea."

"Where's the pea?"

"If I left a piece of pepperoni on the sofa, you would leap into the air."

"At least I know what I think," she said. "Some people go through life with no guidelines whatsoever."

"Do you hear what you sound like? You could be Miss Prissy-Ass, my fifth-grade teacher.

"Is that how you see me?" she said.

"You're too afraid. I want you to be not afraid."

"What a shit-head you are," she said. She was tearful too, tight-mouthed and frowning.

"You don't want to be free?"

"Every sleazebag says that when a woman won't sleep with him."

"Excuse me for offending you," I said.

It went on like that and it didn't get better either. She must have wondered what she was doing with a creep like me. All her innocence, all her young-girl nervousness, made me coarser sometimes.

But all couples had fights, didn't they? Especially when money was in the mix. A day later, Adinah announced that she was taking on more hours in that hippie beanery where she worked, despite my telling her she didn't have to, what was the point.

"I want to. A few extra pennies, okay?"

"You kids are doing so well," my mother said. "It lifts my spirits to talk to you."

Oh, my mother. She still had to see Luís every day at work, which couldn't have been fun, and then—guess what?—my father had turned up at her door, looking like hell and needing a loan, just a little bail-out to tide him over. Which she gave him. I said, "You didn't. Tell me you didn't." And then she wanted to talk to Adinah, and I could hear Adinah saying into the phone, "Generosity is always cool. Name a religion that doesn't say that."

What did my mother know about religion? *Bubkes.* She still had some Yiddish but no theology. What I really wanted to hear was how my father was doing. "He's okay but he's a mess," my mother said. "He always was but now he looks it."

Afterward, Adinah and I talked about whether the truth would out, no matter what, once you got older; whether your physical form stopped being able to hide a thing. Plenty of older people lied to themselves—perky movie stars and oily politicians, sure of their charm and persuasiveness, sure their expensive plastic surgery actually worked—but their faces were so *obvious.* I myself was hiding a few things from the past (Adinah didn't know all) and hoped to someday become the entirely straightforward figure I only half resembled now.

And what about Adinah? In some ways she was guileless—she told customers at work which items were overpriced, she announced, "I just farted," when we were on the bus—but she was also veiled and silent. Often. And why not?

Why shouldn't she keep some of her to herself? I wanted us
both to have privacy.

In May, we celebrated a year in our fantabulous apartment
by having a picnic in Golden Gate Park. We'd both spent
time in the park at antiwar demonstrations and it was somehow especially sweet to be using it for a more idle purpose. I
was halfway through a surprisingly delicious spiced tempeh
sandwich when Adinah said, "You know, I think I might be
pregnant."

Her little tendrils of hair were gleaming in the sun, and I
thought, *She looks about twelve, it's not possible.* (When was
her last period? I couldn't fucking remember. And did I know
when she used her diaphragm? I did not.) Mostly I thought:
What? "Are you sure?" I said.

Everything in her face changed. "Forget I mentioned it,"
she said. "Never mind."

I wanted to forget about it. I didn't want to deal with it
until I absolutely had to. In college one of my girlfriends had
had an abortion. That was kind of normal. Adinah wasn't
normal; she was from the planet of pure feelings, a place
with a molten core.

She was packing up the picnic stuff, the paper cups and
the thermos and the box of chocolate cupcakes we hadn't
eaten. She was getting up to leave.

"Adinah!" I said.

"Never mind," she said. She had the loaded tote bag over
her arm.

"Sit down. Hey. We're talking," I said. "We're talking."

When she sat down, I said, "So how do you feel?" as if I were some kind of goddamn counselor. I knew how she felt.

Oh, she'd guessed for a few weeks, so she'd had time (she said, making her voice go quieter) to get used to the idea that this was *supposed* to happen. What did that mean, "supposed to"? My father believed in the great hand of fate and look where it got him. "What about free will?" I said.

"Stop it," she said.

I could soften, if I wanted, or I could harden myself against her. I saw I could go either way, and I didn't want to go anywhere. I could imagine myself single once more, back in the world as the stone-hearted person I probably really was. I didn't exactly want to picture a baby (boy or girl?). Especially one I might argue to abort.

"I'll have it with or without you, you know," she said.

"Give me time," I said, which enraged her.

But she did wait—where was she going?—while I tormented myself with the prospect of deserting her. We didn't even talk during these days. When I came out of it, as if I'd been fasting, I saw clearly. I was staying for this. Who was I kidding?

I thought Adinah would never entirely emerge from being mad at me, but she mostly did. Twenty times a day we said to each other, *We'll be fine* and *It'll be so great*. By the time we got to, *Timothy if it's a boy and Rebecca if it's a girl*, the shock of it felt like a drug I liked.

One of her friends said that Adinah looked like a deer when she was pregnant. Her small, deep-eyed face, her slender arms and legs, the swelling bodily curve of her. She carried herself nimbly, with that slight sway she developed. I was the galumphing mate, trucking in supplies, fixing up the room. She nagged me about getting the shelves just right.

Adinah's parents did not react well when she tried to begin by first telling them she was living with this guy who was me. Whatever they said (she didn't want to tell me) was so scathing, so full-tilt, so heavy-duty, that she halted the conversation right there and decided not to speak to them again. Ever? "You have no idea," she said. We had a nondenominational wedding, with a bunch of great Sufi musicians really wailing, and my wildly enthusiastic mother in attendance.

I had maybe four good years with Adinah. Becky the baby was a trip, as we kept saying. We didn't know what hit us, but some of it was great. I was one of those fathers who couldn't stop photographing her every yawn and tiny toenail. Adinah was used to kids—she was the oldest of six—and she got strong and fussy in a way I hadn't expected. In one of the pictures I took then she looked like a pioneer mother, chin up, apron on, babe tucked into the crook of her arm.

We tried bringing Becky with us to our Sufi group—Adinah wanted to show how cute she was—but the kid took an immediate dislike to the music, and Adinah had to take her outside when she started bawling. Adinah looked martyred and dismal, standing in the hall jiggling the baby against her shoulder. So I made the noble gesture of staying home with Becky on the nights Adinah felt a need to retune her consciousness to the eternal. I was sort of lapsing out of Sufism by then anyway.

Around this time, I talked Adinah into letting me photograph her stepping out of the tub. Nothing lurid, but I
took the film to a friend's darkroom, no Kodak lab for these.
"I look so pale," Adinah said when she saw them, but she
liked them, I could tell. They had the abstraction of black-
and-white, and in the arcs and mounds and dimplings, the
blurred aureoles and dusky triangle, Adinah's personal flesh
was elevated, made marble. We were otherwise in a morass
of baby poop and bananas and spit-up. We never went out,
what would we pay a sitter with? Our sex life was still okay,
more than okay, but not all that frequent, and the pictures
did us good, they felt like proof. I may have needed them
more than Adinah did.

At my office I was such a pest with my baby portraits
that some supervisor decided I should go photograph clients,
to show them working productively at the jobs we'd nagged
them into getting. I loved this assignment—J. Perez putting
a pizza in the oven, A. LaMarca sticking her butt out to lean
across a file cabinet, X. Jones leading the hokey-pokey at a
day-care center. When a neighborhood newspaper picked
up some of the day-care shots, I was so thrilled that I kept
bothering the editor to buy more photos of mine. A million
stories in the naked city. I got a great one of two guys fighting over their place in line at an Elvis memorial—eyes wild,
jackets flailing, and they both had Elvis hairdos—and this
was such a hit that a real newspaper (a major paper, if not
our best) bought it, and eleven months later I talked them
into a staff job.

I had two things going for me: I knew how to handle
myself on the street and I had enough cool to move in fast for

a shot and get it before it was gone. Sometimes they sent me out with the police reporter, when they needed someone in a hurry. Blood and gore. Me, holding my flashing camera over a facedown body, with cops all around making terrible jokes. All in a day's work.

Adinah hated hearing my stories. "Don't *tell* me about it," she said. "I can't stand it when people get all hip about how close they can get to evil. Like their numbness is something to brag about. It's really kind of revolting."

She had a point, but I had a point too: Didn't she want to know what the world was?

"That isn't *knowledge*," she said. "How can you say that?"

There happened to be any number of women I could show off for if Adinah thought I was full of shit. I flirted with these women, in the newspaper office and on the street, but I didn't, as they say, do anything. I had sold my freedom for love and I was keeping the bargain. I lived with two creatures I loved, didn't I?

Adinah started talking to her parents again. "At least I don't have to put on a midi skirt and long sleeves and a snood over my hair to talk to them," she said. Sometimes she put Becky on the phone. And me. *Hello, Gerard, how are you? Hello, we are fine,* they said. *And a happy holiday to you.* What stiffness in their voices, what years of woe. They were brighter with Becky, whom I could hear gurgling at them. In their photos they looked entirely ordinary and benign—her mother's wig was the same style as Rosalynn Carter's hairdo and her father was smiling under his black plastic eyeglasses, with a yarmulke hardly bigger than a cookie on his balding head. How used to themselves they were, how forever stunned to lose Adinah. In our Sufi group, they had a song with a lot of percussion that was supposed to mean, *The paths of love are long and complicated.* It wasn't human love the song was about either, which made me think all of it was too fucking difficult.

I came home one day with another story from work. A sanitation cop went to give a storekeeper a ticket for illegal garbage on the street, and the big bag of garbage turned out to be the guy's wife, wrapped in plastic, sleeping off a drunk in the rain. A wife he hadn't seen in five years! I got a shot of her standing up and waving like the queen. Adinah said, "That's pretty sad. You don't think that's funny, do you?"

"*I* don't," I said.

"The other guys did."

"Oh, yeah. They're still laughing."

"I knew it."

"I like my work," I said. "Do you mind?"

I knew she'd hate that story, so why did I parade it? She sighed. She'd taken to not bothering to argue with me, which wasn't a good sign.

I was plenty attracted to certain other women—there was a reporter on the paper who reminded me of Sandie, a fast-talking redhead with a very great body. When we were hanging out at the coffee machine, giving each other the eye, I'd think, *It's not worth it, I don't want to make a mess of everything, I have Adinah.*

• • •

In the end it was Adinah who left me. Not for a man, but for a name. In her Sufi group she took on a spiritual guide (you were supposed to do this), a woman in her forties whom Adinah called Tasnim, which meant "Spring of Paradise." Her real name was Carolyn (all the initiates had names their guides gave them) and she was a plumpish woman with a soft voice and blinking eyes. I'd met her at the group long ago, and it surprised me that Adinah picked someone so uncharismatic. Adinah said I'd always gone to Sufism as another drug, a way to cultivate certain states. So was that wrong? "You didn't want to go very far," Adinah said.

She was right that I didn't buy the God part. "Well, that's the whole thing," Adinah said. "And it's not like a single Person. It's the whole Big Enchilada that everything else is inside of. You know?"

I was still interested in this, but I'd stopped needing it. I didn't have the same hunger to get out of myself, now that my days ran on act-first-think-later and blood-and-guts and what felt like success. I was a fair-weather friend to religion. Adinah thought I was shallow.

I was not happy to know this, but we'd always had ups and downs. All the work of taking care of Becky could make our bed a place more for sleep than for love, but sometimes Adinah had gorgeous revivals of feeling. If I was patient, if I could wait while she got our girl to sleep, if she wasn't too tired, a deeper hunger swelled in her. The frank physicality of motherhood seemed to take her to new frontiers. *Lucky me*, I'd thought. Okay, then some long lulls took hold of us. Nothing newsworthy in that. And for some time I was doing the male version of going through the motions. My body rose to excitement, but the rest of me didn't much care. I kept on because I wanted the form of it, I wanted us to be following the ways of a family. As far as I knew, Adinah (who must've noticed) moved with me in that spirit. I thought we agreed.

The Sufi name her guide gave her was Satya, which meant "Sincere" or "Truthful." "Yes!" I said. "You are. That's a great name."

Someone with this name, Adinah thought, wasn't someone who could live in our house. What?

"We live in a house of fake feeling," Adinah said. "You have to pretend every day to hold anything I say in any regard at all."

"*You* don't listen to *me!*" I said, not intelligently.

"If I do, it's to humor you."

"Very nice."

"You don't even bother to humor me," she said

"You want me to say, *Yes, I do?*"

There was a bad pause. "This isn't the way to live," she said. "By lying. I have to tell you, I'm going."

"Go," I said.

I didn't mean it, not really. I said it out of hardness—*Go if you're going*—but I wanted us to stay together. I seemed to want many things. I wanted Becky, who was still in her twos, to cuddle up with me; I wanted Adinah to be with me on life's highway; I wanted to patrol the world of cruelty with my mighty lens; I wanted the old side of my sexual nature to be free again.

What did Adinah want? Not me. She was stuck on the notion of me as bogus and false and fake, as well as loutish and unsuitable. I was in the way of what she hoped to be. How had we ever started? She said I wasn't much of a father anyway, and maybe she was right. We said things we never should have said, and in the end I was the one who left the premises. Out of the Door and down in the street all alone. I had Becky on weekends. She cried when I came to take her with me and she cried when I dropped her off. Why were we doing this? Who was happier?

And Adinah wasn't above making extra demands about money, inventing things they couldn't do without. "Don't act so surprised at what stuff costs," she said.

"I thought you were such a good Sufi," I said.

"We think the world is *real*," she said. "You never got any of this right. It's all God, but veiled. I don't know why I'm even talking to you about it."

"Because I'm Mr. Moneybags," I said. Becky was throwing her wooden blocks at my knees while we spoke. "Cut it out," I said. "Right now." How could we go on this way?

We got used to it. Becky had her own room in the apartment I had in the Haight, a room with a pink record player and a dollhouse. She called me Daddy Dad Dad in case I forgot who I was. Adinah had a Sufi college student, a nice girl with an early version of punk hair, move in to help with the rent, although I was covering most of it, and she got work as a dog walker, which didn't pay that badly.

I took up with the redhead at work—why not?—and I at least had my head always flooded with erotic afterimages. It startled me to be charged with so much sensation at the will of someone so other—I hardly knew her, compared to Adinah—and I was newly amazed by the mystery of these reactions. She had another boyfriend somewhere herself, so we had a good understanding.

Once I was late to pick up Becky because of her, and another time I actually forgot it was my night and I didn't show up. How could I forget? I was too unfeeling and selfish to be anyone's father. I lived in this truth for a month and stayed away—I yelled back at Adinah when she phoned, I wouldn't take her calls at work, I experimented with being a total prick. Why pretend different? And then (when I woke up in sudden anguish) I begged to see Becky again, and Adinah let me. I guess she had to. I was so glad to see her, my Becky with her fat cheeks. But things were always a little fucked up after that.

At work I did a feature with a reporter who wrote about the resourcefulness of the homeless. I had been waiting for an assignment like this. I got shots of a man who'd trained his dog to panhandle with a cup tied to its paw, a guy in a wheelchair who'd rigged up a Mylar umbrella for an awning, a mother washing dandelion greens in a fountain to feed to her kids. I kidded around, I thanked them for their time. Some of them wanted a little payment—which we weren't supposed to give as journalists—and some of them were embarrassed by all of it.

The photos had respect in them, I didn't make them cloying. I could do that much. Adinah said, "Excellent work," which pleased me greatly. She of all people could see why I wanted to remind the public that the unmoneyed were actually real humans.

She looked trim and healthy these days, in her jeans and her striped polos, with more color in her face. All that dog-walking was doing her good. Oh, yes, she was thinking of branching out and starting her own walking service. Adinah as an entrepreneur? "Not just me," she said. "With someone."

Her co-walker was a guy named Marty, who answered the door to the apartment one morning when I showed up—a tall guy with hair like a big black mop. Okay, I didn't like him, how could I? Becky was clambering all over him, giggling. He was no mere business acquaintance. Adinah was still in her bathrobe. "Morning, man," he said to me. He called Adinah "Deen," he called Becky "Beck." Who the hell did he think he was?

"You think you're going to get rich leading mutts around?" I asked Adinah. "You think there's big bucks in dog shit?"

And he was there almost every time I came by. In her days with me, Becky liked to talk about how Marty could whistle any tune, how Marty told her stories about all the dogs. Itchy and Doodlehound and Fatface, he called them. I was paying rent so this sucker could sleep in my bed? Adinah said, "What do you care? He doesn't live here." If he ever moved in, I didn't see it, because I had trouble showing up as often.

It just wasn't very pleasant to see how the waters had closed over what had once been my spot.

I got offered a job in New York, a city I always liked, and it was better for everyone this way. I had Becky in the summers. Not every summer (I said no a few times) and not all summer, but we had a great August in the Catskills when she was six and she really liked her Brooklyn day camp when she was eight and she was in a great help-clean-up-the-parks program when she was in middle school.

When Becky was twelve, Adinah switched to another Sufi group—she liked the leader better, he gave great talks, they had better music—and this group had kept its ties with Islam. My ex-wife was becoming a Muslim! "It's kind of great," she said. Fine with me. So when Becky spent her summers with me, did she have to be taken to a mosque? There was some discussion of this—was there even the right kind of mosque anywhere near me? actually, there was—and finally Becky was asked what she wanted, which was to be exclusively in Dad-land when she was with Dad. Later for the Sufis.

A girlfriend I had at the time was spooked by the mosque thing. "So what are they telling your kid in there? And she has a Jewish father! Do they even know that?" That girlfriend didn't last long. I did try to ask Becky what they were telling her in there. "Oh, you know," she said. "The Unity of Being stuff. Opening the heart. The old usual." She seemed to just take it for granted, one more thing the grown-ups invented. "And there's prayers, of course." What she liked to do with me was go to Burger King, since cheeseburgers were not served at home. We went to horror movies together too, a favorite illicit activity. And she had friends from her park camp, nice girls from what our mayor liked to call the gorgeous mosaic of our diverse city.

What did I really think? Part of me thought Adinah was just filling her vacant life (the Marty guy was long gone, the dog-walking had to be a job with limited satisfactions) and part of me envied her. I was a serious person in my own way, but I'd stopped considering the unseen and how to work with it. I didn't have what Adinah had, a capacity for devotion and a thirst to soar, an instinct for flight. I didn't think she was crazy (were a billion Muslims in the world crazy?), but her parents must have thought that, if they even knew. They probably didn't know.

And I'd been to Muslim countries, by this time, once to photograph a famous slum in Cairo and once for a trade conference in Jakarta. In both places I heard by-the-by invectives against Israel and the Jews from locals chatting me up, and I'd kept my mouth shut about being Jewish. Which I later felt creepy about, although as a photojournalist I kept my mouth shut about a lot of things. But would I have been any happier if Adinah had converted to Catholicism or gone to live in an ashram or meditated with the Dalai Lama? The great chasm would still have been there, between the realms where our gazes were fixed. Between us.

Over the years friends had asked if Adinah and I might get back together and I'd always said no. That was over. No pennies left in that piggy bank. We were, of course, tied forever by Becky. Sometimes I had daydreams of us in the same apartment again, back at the Door, and both of us better at it this time. You never forget certain years of being young. Not that I hadn't fallen for other women—I'd had some long intrigues and some very hot flashes-in-the pan—but Adinah turned out to be my big deal. Who knew?

Maybe Adinah was going to meet a nice fellow at the mosque. I knew they sat apart, men and women, but some-body's brother? I tried feeling out Becky on this—were there committees her mom was on, were there bake sales or fes-tivals or fund-raisers? Becky said, "It's too boring for me to know." I said, "I met your mom watching dervishes, did you know that?" "No," she said.

But I was the one who met somebody at a mosque. I was photographing an East Village mosque in a plain storefront building on First Avenue, for an article on flourishing tradi-tions in the Big Apple. They paired me with a reporter named Frances, a go-getter who was very good at chatting up all the Bangladeshi and Bengali cabdrivers who left their shoes on shelves in the hall (I got a good shot of the shoes) before they went in to pray. She had an interview with the council presi-dent, in his endearingly crummy office, and drew out some quotable stuff from a Nigerian woman with five kids and a teenager with parents from Kolkata. Afterward we stuffed ourselves on smoky chicken and onions from the halal food cart across the street. She interviewed the cart guy too, who was Moroccan.

She had short hair that was dyed too streaky and a funny, rough voice. When I said, "This is a lot less trouble than covering the guy who threw his mother down the elevator shaft," she laughed so easily I thought, *Oh, she likes me*. I started telling her about that story—the mother was not a nice person—and she said, "Please. I had the one where a middle school kid stole crack from a teacher." The conversation seemed very comradely to the two of us.

She was closer to my age than I'd thought at first. She had a son older than Becky, she'd grown up in Staten Island, she had a brother who was a priest, and by the time I drove us back to the newsroom, we both knew something was starting between us.

Frances was my big stroke of luck. She was not simple to be with (full of opinions she wouldn't let rest), and during our first six months together she could never stay over because her boy was still in high school, but she was my best idea yet of who to love. Even Becky, who took a whole summer to come around, said, "Frances knows what's going on." Aside from her sex appeal, Frances was what my mother used to call a good egg. Once we got over some of the initial stupidities and misfirings, we were kind of dazzling as a couple.

It wasn't until the fourth year, when we actually moved in together, that Frances found herself talking to Adinah on the phone. The women were entirely civil and friendly, two rational beings—what did they have to fight over?—as they discussed

Becky's plane reservations from California. Dogs were barking in the background, Frances told me later, yap yap yap. Adinah provided home boarding, for extra bucks, when she could.

"Doesn't the Koran have something against dogs?" Frances said.

"Not the Koran itself. Not at all. And she says there are different traditions," I said.

Frances did give me a look that said, *She's so odd*, but it wasn't a mean look.

As it happened, I was stuck way up in East Harlem, shooting some cop talking about retirement benefits, when the World Trade Center was smashed to rubble by two planes. Once I could get through to Frances to make sure she was okay, once I called my mother in Florida to tell her I was fine, once they started flashing pictures of Osama bin Laden on the TV monitors at work, I kept thinking I had to get to California to protect Adinah and Becky from anti-Muslim bigots. They were sitting ducks, my girls. Becky was out of school and living at home, back at the Door till she could find a job. When I finally got Adinah on the phone, she said, "Oh! We were so worried about you. It's so great to hear you're all right. You're all right?"

"Please be careful," I said. "Don't parade around being a Muslim right now, okay?"

"Careful how?" she said. "Do you think there's a lynch mob in the streets?"

"I don't like to think of the two of you alone," I said.

"Becky's out with the dogs now. And the mosque is fine too. I was just there. No problems."

"You were where?"

"Of course. Everyone came. It was very moving."

"You took Becky with you?" I said. "What's the matter with you?"

Adinah said Becky was twenty-three and could make her own decisions. "I'm not *bringing* her anyplace. I have to tell you, you're thinking about this in entirely the wrong way. I know you want to guard us, but how? It's kind of a grandiose idea about yourself. This is what happens to people's egos without religion."

"Oh, is it?"

"I'm sorry to say it is."

"This isn't such a great week for religion," I said.

"In my house it is," she said.

"You know how you sound?"

"I hate it when you're an asshole," she said.

One of the photos I took at that time won a prize (a cop in a paper air-filter mask reading a wall of those early, futile posters for the missing). It wasn't hard to catch a long, sad story in an instant during those days, and I was, first and foremost, a street photographer. My mother was so pleased about my getting a prize she talked about it nonstop. There were a lot better photos than the one I took, and I envied the people who got to the scene fast enough. "I wouldn't tell anyone about this envy if I were you," Frances said.

I always wanted to be out in the world, taking in as much as I could take, and was this now creepy of me? Should I be mourning and not staring? The newsroom lost its rowdy, smart-alecky din around this time—people were stricken, solemn, formal. Reverent without a focus. We really didn't know how to act. We reached for what we could reach for.

In the middle of the next summer I got an email from Adinah. *Hope you're well and keeping out of trouble. I have a small request*, she wrote. Like every Muslim who was able, she was called to make the hajj, the trip to Mecca. Some families from her mosque were going in February. Becky would take care of the dogs, the one thing she needed was permission. (She needed what?) I was still her legal husband. It was a simple consent form, I just had to sign, no big deal, she would send it to me. She was also short on money to pay for the trip, if I wanted to kick in, but that was up to me.

My first thought was: *She'll be killed*. They would find out she was Jewish. She was out of her mind, this present-day Adinah, and the fact of that was extremely painful to me. A deluded fifty-two-year-old woman, walking right out into traffic, too helpless to live in this world.

"How would they know what she was born as?" Frances said. "Americans go on this thing all the time."

Frances was just talking. I looked at my newspaper's files online. I could find nothing at all about murders in Mecca. There hadn't been any riots or bombs since the eighties, but the hajj did have a history of accidental stampedes. In 1990 there had been a rush inside a pedestrian tunnel between Mecca and Mina and 1,426 pilgrims had died. In some other years only a hundred or so were trampled. A few dozen had died this year from meningitis, and there were always deaths from heat prostration. And at the end of the hajj, there was a ritual sacrifice, a massive slaughter of sheep, goats, and cows, on behalf of the pilgrims. Most of the butchered flesh went to the poor, but how could a woman who hadn't eaten meat since 1971 be up for this?

It gave me some degree of comfort that I could stop her. I could do that for her, at least, after all these years. *Adinah, you don't have a clue what you're getting into,* I wrote. *Did you really think I or anyone with a brain would go along with this? It's too insane. Sorry to be a party pooper, but that's my opinion.*

You think you're saving me, don't you? Adinah wrote back. *What a full-of-yourself jerk you are. You have everything backward. This is why Muslims go around saying only God is God. Get over yourself, okay? Soon.*

Frances said, "It's bad enough she has to *ask* you—and you're saying no? I don't believe you."

Frances was very chilly to me, and she meant it—I had appalled her—and work was no picnic that week either. I was with a reporter who was covering the case of a couple who'd beaten the woman's four-year-old son to death. We interviewed the grandmother, the neighbors, the social worker, the usual, and I hated hearing the details. Some grisly bits were hard to forget. Even the reporter, a hard-boiled guy, was pretty quiet afterward. I was angry that these facts, true as they were, had entered me. The writer and I got drunk together standing at a bar, downing shots of whiskey, old-style city-desk guys.

· · ·

That night I dreamed of Becky when she was maybe three, right after I first moved out, and she was pouncing on my back the way she used to when I read the paper at night. In my dream, I turned around and smacked her. As I once really had. In the dream, she was riding around on the back of a huge black dog, shrieking like a bird of prey in a horror movie, a vicious sound.

Frances was asleep next to me when I woke up, in murky terror. I thought, *It's too hard, I can't stand it*, though I couldn't have said what that meant. What I really thought was, a person shouldn't remember too much.

I stayed in the shower for a half hour the next morning, my version of all the ritual washing that religions go in for. I once saw a Muslim prayer room at an airport, where there was a spigot for ablutions. In the steam of the shower when I came out, I didn't want to look in the mirror either. I hoped black coffee would help, and maybe it did.

I had a hangover all day, a bad one, and I kept thinking about Adinah, how she had every right to go to Mecca or wherever the hell she wanted, I'd known that all along. There wasn't enough mercy in the world. Let her go, let her be one of those pilgrims in the baking sun. It was entirely like her to want such a thing. And millions of people went to Mecca every year and came home fine. Every year.

But I put off writing to her that I'd had a change of heart. I walked around with my heart as it was, unsightly and hidden.

I had to work my butt off and run all over the city as usual, aiming my camera at suspects holding their jackets over their heads and lawyers acting earnest. All of this made me more infuriated with Adinah. She always thought she was above all this crap, too good to go near it. But she wanted a hand-out from me anyway, extra bucks for her voyage into the sky, which she couldn't even afford.

I slept, I ate, I seeped into stoniness. It wasn't so bad either. Frances ignored me. I didn't care what she thought. I didn't care about anything. My email had no more messages from Adinah—I was glad of that—but Becky wrote. *Mom doesn't even ask for anything and she's saved all her money for this. What's the matter with you?* and I didn't answer.

I might've walked around like that forever, not bothering with anything, but I stopped being good at it. I forgot one day when I walked onto a subway platform with Frances, and the ancient, loudmouth bum who hadn't been there for a while was yelling, "Help the winos! Support your local wino! Remember the winos of New York!" This cracked me up, despite the many times I'd heard it before, and I saw that I missed being human. The bum said, "Hah, got a smile out of you," a sentence I have always hated, and I didn't even mind.

Okay, okay, I wrote to Adinah. *Sorry for the delay.*

Only Muslims are allowed to enter Mecca and Medina. Adinah had a paper from the imam of her mosque saying she was a real one, and a travel agent got her the visa. She'd never even had a passport before! And here she was, heading for Saudi Arabia, a pink-skinned middle-aged white lady who spoke nothing but English. She was training for the rigors, she said, by running a mile or so every day; dog-walking was good exercise but not that good. Becky reported her buying things to wear—a bunch of white cotton caftans and head scarves for the ritual walking, and a few blue ones (she always liked blue) for the rest of the time, since women had to be covered in public in Saudi Arabia. "She looks so weird in her *abaya*," Becky said. "I can't believe it's Mom. Don't tell her I said that."

She was studying the prayers. Adinah said to me, "I'm so excited I can't stand it."

Hadn't she had other excitements? What about the time we cracked the headboard during delirious, athletic sex? What about when Becky was born and Adinah couldn't get over her really, really being our own girl? What about the day she thought I was dead in the World Trade Center and then I wasn't?

Frances said, "It's the whole city of God versus the city of man thing."

The what?

"Oh, you know. Saint Augustine thought history was a running battle between the two. Heavenly beauty of purpose versus earthly preoccupations. Guess which was going to win in the end?"

"You'd think a person could live in both," I said.

"Augie didn't think so," she said.

Frances knew quite a bit about saints, if you got her going, though she wasn't a believer. She was temperamentally like me, nose to the grindstone of the here-and-now. How sensible we were, compared to that nut job Adinah.

•   •   •

And Becky, who had a perfectly good job assisting the editor of a knitting magazine, was going to take a two-week leave from it so she could walk one pack of dogs after another up and down the steep hills of San Francisco. Her mother (who hardly had a dime to her name) had to leave for the hajj free of debts and with her financial responsibilities covered. So her devoted daughter had to pick up dog poop while Adinah in her white robes glided off into the desert? Was that the way of it?

It was. I might have bought a ticket to California and just walked the dogs myself—I liked dogs, actually, and when I was a kid, my father was always going to get me one—or I might have paid someone to take Becky's place—I could handle the amount, whatever it was, and wouldn't that be financially handsome of me? I thought about both these things. Frances would've been horrified if I'd done either of them, but that wasn't what stopped me. What stopped me was that *it wasn't like me*. Skipping out on my job to lurch through the streets with a leash of panting mutts, mailing a large, unasked-for check to a woman I hadn't slept with for more than two decades: not what I did.

I vowed that I would phone Becky often, to make sure she was okay and to get any news of Adinah. But I was in the middle of shooting a series about security guards in city schools, and I lost track of when the whole Mecca thing was, until I noticed stuff on the video monitors at work. Al Jazeera was broadcasting in English. "That's my wife!" I said.

The whole room turned around to look at me. What we were watching, viewed from above, was a speckled mass, flecked white and gray, that was actually a sea of people, circling and pulsating around the giant black cube that was the Kaaba, the sacred site within the mosque. The spots of dark and light kept changing as the sea that was people kept moving, slow as a dream, stately, terrifying, constant.

My coworkers watching the monitor kept looking back at me to see if I was a Muslim and they'd never noticed. "She's not really my wife," I said.

They were ready to make wisecracks but I had scared them. I was busy thinking, *Let her be okay.* I had to wonder then who I was asking. The TV cut to an outside shot of the mosque, domes and minarets of gleaming pale stone, with more fields of humans pouring in. I stayed to watch, I had a horse in this race.

It occurred to me that the people winding around the Kaaba at the moment were really quite ordinary people. No better than I was, probably. But right now they were better. On TV a cheerful Punjabi pilgrim was showing the two pieces of regulation white cloth all the men wore—and what a pain it was to keep the top piece wrapped over your shoulder so you weren't bare-chested. I would certainly look like a total idiot in that getup. I realized I was imagining myself in it.

In what life could I have ended up as a pilgrim? When could I have been someone who walked all that far, miles and miles, to visit innocence in the form of a place? Alongside me now by the video monitor the guys at work were yukking it up about the pilgrims' white cloths. Easy to clean but not good for the office. I had the oddest feeling then—I was entirely glad that I'd known Adinah. As if I could wave to her from my side of the TV screen, *Hi, girl.* As if we were parts of the same body, as married couples dream of being, one shadow of us in the desert, another shadow in the newsroom. It was a very airy idea I had—and not one I could hold on to very long—but I kept it with me while I went about my business, while I did the job I knew how to do, I kept it all day and it was mine.

Buying and Selling

It still could startle Rudy, after all this time, to think how much of his working life involved courting the favor of rich people, coaxing them to donate a little bit of what they had plenty of. Who could begin to guess how many, many things depended on some rich fuck being generous? Hospitals! Orchestras! Universities! Homes for the homeless, food for the hungry. Rehab for rape victims, help for the lepers of India. Small wonder the deep pockets of the world couldn't keep from complaining that some moocher always had a hand out.

Rudy worked for one of those hands—he worked for the lepers, in fact—and he had never meant to do such a thing. How had it happened? He'd been a New York club kid as a teenager, a serious fan of high-noise music who hung out in dives with ever-changing deejays all over the five boroughs. He'd lurched through his years at Columbia, barely getting up for classes but demonically intent when writing papers. And then he'd had the entirely insane idea to go into investment banking. Lots of aimless youth were doing that then. He was hired because people generally liked him, and he was put to work computer-crunching, culling data for analysis. After he'd spent a year turning into a gloomy creep with a good salary, one of the senior bankers took him to a meeting in Kuala Lumpur, and he was so happy roaming the streets in the evenings—night markets! mosques! the once-tallest building in the world!—that he decided he could quit and travel dirt-cheap if he wanted, who would stop him?

And he did fine as a backpacker, good at guessing what was going on, dazzled by newness, skilled at scrimping. He made friends easily, he picked up bits of languages, he was only sick a few times and never robbed. He liked just about all of it—Thailand, Malaysia, Sumatra, Sri Lanka—until he got to India.

The thing about India was that people did not ever, ever leave you alone. Not just the poor women holding their babies out, the begging toddlers pointing to their mouths, the old men without shoes or shirts or much flesh on their bodies, whom he could hardly blame for wanting to shake him down for what they could, and not just the hustlers of DVDs or instant tailoring or very-nice-girls or bargain rubies, who had to make a living. But also the schoolboys who entertained themselves imitating him to each other, the brightly bossy ones who couldn't let him read a map without telling him what he really had to see.

As a New Yorker, Rudy was already a little too used to being hard-hearted, which at least made him unafraid of misery. He did give change if he thought he could avoid being swarmed. But every day, just when he thought he understood the place, he was duped or refuted or told silly lies. How did people live here? He decided that religion—apparent everywhere, in the ornate and amazing temples, in the marks of vermilion or ash or sandalwood paste on people's faces—was the really interesting thing in India. On the advice of a couple at his hostel, he took a long, hot bus ride out of Mumbai to the city of Nasik, where the sacred Godavari River flowed. He arrived in the hottest part of the day, and he saw right away his mistake about religion here—not peaceful at all! not quiet! The closer he got to the river, the more the roadways swarmed with visitors, with wandering sadhus with painted faces and chests, with the wrecked and injured and alarming. At the river, women beat bright silk laundry against the rocks, boys goofed around in rented rowboats, and pilgrims waded into the stream. Sellers of bracelets, fried foods, incense, and postcards of Hindu gods leaped forward at the sight of Rudy.

He was making his way from this scene, up a narrow path on the bank, when a beggar with a bowl on a chain around his neck stopped him. The man, whose face looked strangely dried, with patches of lighter skin across the cheeks and neck, held out his curled hands, to show that some fingers were rounded nubs, missing the bits past the knuckle. *Oh, God, he's a leper,* Rudy thought. *Is that what he is?* When he got out his wallet—he was wildly relieved he had a small bill on him, not too big to give—the man gazed in rheum-eyed thanks.

At the time, Rudy only wanted to get out of Nasik as soon as he could. He left the next day for Pune, where he took up with a pretty and fearless Englishwoman, who led them to the beaches of Goa, where he stayed for a month. But Nasik marked the beginning of chewing over a problem. He knew he wasn't equal to doing anything very pure. On the other hand, there were lepers.

He certainly had not expected to stay in India; he didn't even like it. But in Chennai he met this sweet, hilarious girl (Berry, a redhead from Miami), who was volunteering in a school for street kids, and she enlisted him in getting the boys to run off some of their energy in the tiny yard. This was not so hard, once he got his iPod hooked up with speakers and blasted some music for them to move to. He gave them his favorite tunes and he downloaded some Tamil pop and Bollywood numbers in Hindi. The boys had their own moves (signs of the ancient roots of hip-hop) and worked up some giddy routines.

It was no big deal to video it and put it on the school's website. Rudy was home, back in New York, by the time it got posted—Berry wrote and said everyone noticed that donations were doubling and tripling, millions of rupees were pouring in. She was kidding, but he half believed her because it was so cool.

Back in New York (what an expensive city), he fudged a little on a job application and cited his fund-raising experience in Chennai. And so it went; he was hired by an excellent liberal arts college (his druggiest friend had gone there) to join the development staff. He turned out to be so good at inspiring donors to cough up cash that he then made a lateral move to a bigger college. And now, a decade after he'd gotten into it, he'd taken an absurd pay cut to be the director of understaffed Development for Hansen's Hope, a network of care centers and residences and schools in South Asia for people with Hansen's disease, aka leprosy.

"And it's not *that* contagious," he always had to say. *Hope* was in the name so people didn't shriek and toss the appeals away at once. You had to emphasize the need but not disgust or horrify anyone, always a fine line. There had been a cure for more than two decades, for Christ's sake. Rudy selected photos with interesting faces, not just ravaged figures, for the newsletter, which he mostly wrote. He was new at this, and it was much more of a challenge than getting college alums to send checks to their dear old distinguished schools. You'd think people would want to rain gold on the truly afflicted, but no, *pas du tout*.

HH had been started forty-odd years before by a rich kid back from the Peace Corps, and the board was still mostly friends of his family. Not young, but boards weren't. Rudy got along best with the women and wives—well, that was his nature—and Deedee, one of his favorites, had brought a friend, a new "prospect," to this year's garden party gala in Central Park. Donor prospects were few and far between these days. Quite a handsome woman still, with dark hair pulled back in a bun, pale skin, red lips, the beaded silk suit a little dressy for a garden party. But she was French, they were a dressy people.

So now Rudy was trying to talk her up, without, of course, seeming to do more than bring her a mini-samosa and some punch. Was she from Paris? He had been to Paris. What a city.

She sort of laughed at him. "You will say to me about the croissants you ate. Maybe I like New York better. Do you think I am a traitor?"

Not answering that one. "What do you like about us?" he said.

"People are not acting superior, maybe they think they are but they don't say it."

"But we're not as good-looking as the French," he said.

She gave him a knowing smile. "If I say we have beautiful genes," she said, "I will be acting superior."

Liliane could not remember why she'd agreed to come to this garden party with Deedee. It was true she'd always liked parties, but less and less these days. She hoped she was past the need to parade herself (who wants to be a ridiculous seventy-one-year-old?) and the effort it took to enter conversations around her in English kept making her think, *Why am I listening to some idiot who knows less than I do?*

If you saw through everything, it made it hard to figure out what to do with yourself. This was the dilemma Liliane faced on a daily basis. It wasn't much of a real problem, she knew, compared, for instance, to the constituency served by Hansen's Hope. But it drove her to do things she didn't expect, spend money she didn't have. She had known herself better when she was young.

Her son, Emile, always told her how cynical she was. She was never cynical about *him*, but he knew her opinions on everything else. They were close, in their sometimes combative way. He was in his forties now and lived in the countryside in Limousin. When they Skyped, his ruddy bearded face on the computer was always startling, always dear.

He hadn't had the best childhood either. She'd had him on her own—the pregnancy was an oversight she ignored too long—and it was before the government made such a big point of helping you. She got by on a part-time job guiding English-speaking tourists (bad pay) and on the occasional generosity of boyfriends. Her girlfriends served as babysitters and were highly unreliable. The early years were filled with screaming desperation, and her son remembered some of it. It was her very good luck that when Emile was twelve, she took up with the sheikh. He was not a sheikh at all—that was their own nickname for him, since his family was from Morocco and his name happened to be Ahmed. He'd been born in Paris, in fact, and he owned a nightclub on the edge of Montmartre, which was where Liliane met him. He hired all kinds of musicians, happier with newness than most people are, and it was a cozy, lively spot, moving in and out of prosperity as trends swirled around it. He and Liliane never married (why get into religious tangles?), but they lived together without undue strife for many years. They lived in Liliane's cluttered apartment, and he was out working much of the time, waiting for beverage deliveries or meeting promoters in cafés. She was under the impression that quite a lot of his profits went to his mother, he was the only son, but when Liliane complained of this, they had their one bitter quarrel, and she kept her outrage down after that. Mostly he was a sweet-tempered man, playful, expansive, genuinely clever, good with Emile. He brought her quite beautiful presents— he was a sucker for anything with a lily in its design—and he kept up his admiring patter, his droll, flirtatious praise, in the same rhythms for two decades.

The club had a big resurgence in the nineties—all of a sudden half of Paris wanted to hear some Algerian raï group that had been playing there for years—and lines clogged the street outside. Ahmed, in a display of enterprise she'd hardly seen before, opened another club a few blocks away, which was also packed. Maybe a third club? What a busy, lit-up ringmaster he turned into—in those years he was an over-wrought and entirely happy man. They were both in their fifties by then, and Liliane managed to at least get a better wardrobe out of all his hunches paying off. A black cashmere coat with raglan sleeves, a short red dress by a great designer that looked wonderful on her. She still had them.

He was only sixty when he died, cracking his handsome, beloved head when he fell off a ladder he'd mounted to check out a faulty spotlight. Liliane wailed like an animal when they told her. She could not swallow the impossible stupidity of the accident—he was not a man who should've died at that age. Quick and strong, free of the bad habits of most club owners, tuned to the pleasures of this earth.

His friends—perfectly nice men she'd known for years—said that she really should not go to the funeral, women didn't go to the ceremony. She stayed back in his sister's house (his mother was long gone), helping the women in the family prepare for the visitors who came after. She was too stricken to be indignant, though later at home she heard her-self mutter a few completely idiotic anti-Muslim things to Emile, who said, "Oh, stop. You can, I know." Ahmed had liked his mosque (when he bothered to go), it had great Sufi chanting and singing, but Liliane was raging at everything in those days.

And what was she going to do? The clubs could not go on without Ahmed. She would get by, she always did, but how? Musicians were planning a memorial concert to honor him, and there was talk of raising some money for her as part of this. Before it could happen, a lawyer called her about the will. Ahmed had apparently been putting his profits (what profits?) into real estate. He had left nice sums to his sisters, but there were two buildings in Belleville and a good-sized lot near Orly that were now hers and worth more euros than she could guess. It was the great shock of her life—she was more stunned than if he had been unfaithful for years. He had tricked her, outsmarted her behind her back. Probably he hadn't wanted her to know about the money for fear she would spend it. Well, she would've wanted to. Had he thought he couldn't resist her?

It was not a comfortable mystery, and it was strange being joyous about the money just when she was beaten flat by the weight of constant despair. If death ate everything, could it possibly matter that money had come to her? To Liliane it could. At first she did nothing but cash the checks from the rents when an agent sent them. How illicit it felt, how underhanded the glee of the money seemed. As if she were a spy, impersonating Ahmed's wife, when he didn't have a wife. A well-paid spy.

"I feel like an impostor," she said to Emile.

"Some people like that feeling," Emile said. He was not such a person—this was why he lived in the country and sold cheeses for a living—but he was not an innocent.

Liliane knew very little about managing property, but she learned what she could and she believed she had more sense than most people. In time she turned into the harder sort of boss (this did not surprise her), with an eye out for corruption, wily enough in hiring contractors, raising rents, firing the lazy, and sneaking around certain taxes. Later she sold the Orly piece at what turned out to be a very opportune time.

None of this was what newspapers would call big money, but it was to Liliane, who came from a family of bricklayers. In France no one ever mistook her for well connected, and she was amused when she and Emile took a trip to Antibes, and some Americans at the hotel assumed her style was aristocratic. Emile thought it was because they heard him telling her how he missed the sheikh. Liliane ended up befriending one of the Americans anyway, a tiny, hearty woman who told funny stories at breakfast, and they all went together to hear jazz outside at night. Deedee, the woman, had decent taste in music.

And Liliane was very glad she had Deedee to spend some days with, in this month of vacation she was giving herself in New York. They got along very well, despite Deedee's immensely comical notion that Liliane was a woman who went to balls and benefits. "No one has money anymore," Deedee could say, and she meant people had two hundred million instead of three hundred. Something like that.

Liliane herself had lost quite a bit in the "*crise*"—it wasn't such a good time to be in real estate after all. Her attempts to recoup had been especially disastrous. She'd come here (she'd always liked Americans) as a very necessary break from the vice of buying and selling and putting her money in the wrong places. The last months had shaken her confidence. She was thinking about more travel now, on the theory she might as well spend it before it disappeared on its own. Emile wouldn't care what he was left. Or did everyone always care?

This party for Deedee's charity was in a very beautiful garden, an enclave of formal greenery near 105th Street, quite unlike the rest of New York. Worth seeing, certainly. It had allées of fruit trees and grassy terraces and a fountain of dancing bronze maidens. The boy was saying, "People get married here, although I wouldn't say it was a really sexy garden."

"Who is saying that a wedding must have to be sexy?" Liliane said.

"I've never been married myself. I bow to your greater knowledge," he said.

Liliane gave him a look. The boy had a good head, squarish and somehow graceful, with brownish hair gelled back from his forehead.

"I was married in a mosque," she said.

Generally, people switched the subject when you mentioned mosques. He asked if he could get her more punch, another tidbit?

Deedee came by when she was alone. "We did well, I'm very happy," she said. "Look how many people. For a great cause."

A woman behind them wore a lovely, broad-brimmed straw hat, trimmed with whimsical flowers. She certainly didn't look as if she were thinking about lepers, but why should she be? Weren't her dollars worth more than thoughts? Liliane was of that opinion, although she hadn't always been.

The boy was back with an Indian sweetmeat, a delicious lump of what he said was chickpea flour and sugar and clarified butter. "I totally stuffed myself on these when I was living in India," he said.

"Did you like it there?" she asked.

"No and yes. It's mind-boggling. You have to keep five hundred contradictions in your head at once to even pay attention there."

Liliane was starting to like him better.

"Don't even ask how many calories these have," Deedee said. "But you don't have to worry."

"She certainly doesn't," Rudy said. "It's a French secret, isn't it? I think they *are* a superior race."

Rudy lingered with his assistant, Veena, after the guests were gone and the caterers were folding up the chairs. "Success!" she said. "Good turnout."

"These things cost too much money," he said. "Low profit. We're not a big outfit."

"Oh, we're always in a squeeze. What else is new?"

"Yes," Rudy said. "Mighty me. I'll carry us all."

His oldest friends would've laughed themselves silly at his carrying anyone anywhere. They thought he was a doofus in a suit, a slacker who'd managed to disguise himself as employed. Little did they know he was a professional. Who wants to be conned by a sharpie? No, the modest young fellow is the one you want to write a check to. That was what *disarming* meant: didn't know what hit you.

He used to bring his girlfriends to galas, and they had liked dressing up and getting the glamour of it. He was just as glad he was single at the moment. Liliane was going to require undistracted attention. She was arch and wary (how had she captured the sheikh?), an unlikely pal for Deedee, and he didn't have long to cultivate her.

His boss, Mary the Figurehead, was now stepping across the grass to literally pat him on the head. She was a bulky, mild-voiced woman in beige linen. "Well done," she said.

"Oh, you say that to all the boys," Rudy said. It was never a mistake to flirt just slightly with her. She was chief executive, though most of the decisions were made on the ground without her, in India and Bangladesh.

"I'm always so glad you're with us," she said, which was bullshit, it was just the way she talked.

HH was not in good shape, in truth. In South Asia, the rainy season was just starting again. Last year's flooding rains had washed out no less than four of the organization's centers, and the rebuilding wasn't anywhere near finished on three of them. His email was full of pleas from the managers, piles of painful details, as if *he* were the one to persuade. *Please do not forget us*, they liked to say.

One of Rudy's girlfriends had referred to what he did as "a high-stress job," and he'd ditched her after that. *Dear managers, your pesky suffering is so stressing me out.* Right. All the same, he was probably drinking more since he'd been doing this. And a few other things.

When he left the gala, he walked across the park (how beautiful the last mellow daylight was, he loved his city) to get the Brooklyn-bound subway to his apartment in Fort Greene. There he collapsed on his sofa in front of the news, and when he woke up what felt like many years later, his cell phone said 11:03 p.m., an hour at which there was nothing to do but get up and splash water on his face and go out into the night.

At a bar a few blocks away, he swilled down beer and listened to an okay but not thrilling neo-punk group that blasted out monotonous chants and then broke into a pretty close imitation of the Sex Pistols (he had loved them when he was ten) screeching how they wanted to destroy the passerby 'cause they *wanted to be anarchy*. Surely this wasn't all that was left of the anarchists of the world. This fabulous shrieking. Had anybody occupying Wall Street remembered to sing those songs? He hoped so. Rudy could see why revolution was no longer a faith, but the results of that were not all good, as the Occupiers had pointed out quite eloquently. He sort of hated rich people himself, and he probably saw the best of them.

He left when the band did a loud and louder brain-blitz that didn't feel like pleasure. He was getting too old for this shit. But it was too early to go to bed, and he walked a few blocks to a club that booked untrendy jazz and oddball blues, old-timers and upstarts, a place almost ruined when the *Times* ran a feature on it. So it was mobbed with assholes now, so what? Assholes had a right to like music.

When he walked inside, it was indeed packed. He liked the mixed audience—a Latino kid with an eentsy beard and

a hooded sweatshirt next to a dame from a different neighborhood in pearls (pearls!) and satin slacks. A piano player
who looked six years older than God was doing great things
with "I'm a King Bee."

At the end of the set, people shuffled around, and Rudy
got a good seat at the bar. At a table near him two older
women were cracking each other up as they ordered drinks.
One of them could not seem to pronounce, "One more Rob
Roy on the rocks," and he saw (could this be right?) that her
friend in pearls, laughing away, was Liliane. How had she
gotten here? Was this place in guidebooks now, drawing
Euro-trash? "Hello, hello," he called across to her.

It took her a second to get who he was. "Oh, my friend
from the garden," she said.

"How nice to see you again," he said. "How very, very nice."

Liliane had been having an excellent time. She was with a
truly old friend, an American whom she had known in her
twenties. Barbara had spent a year in Paris as a college student, and for this trip had been miraculously located again
through email by Emile, smart boy that he was. In their
youth the two women had spent many vivid evenings picking
up men together. Barbara remembered quite a few details
that Liliane had mercifully forgotten. The current Barbara
was stringier and paler—Liliane would not have known
her—but as the evening went on, her younger face began
to surface. She had kept something of her looks, in a messy,
New York way.

They were not as drunk as they were acting, but they were

not sober either. Why should they be? Barbara's husband had gone home to sleep, and Liliane kept thinking she saw an ex-lover at one of the tables, an American clarinet player she'd once stolen some cash from. It was never him, and she wasn't even picturing him at what would be his real age, but she kept thinking what she would say if it was. *That money wasn't doing you any good anyway.* He'd been an alcoholic, he was probably dead by now. When last seen, he was playing his clarinet for spare change in the Métro.

"Your friend got this round," the bartender said. He meant the boy from the garden party.

"*Très gentil.*" Liliane saluted him in thanks.

Barbara introduced herself. "I knew Liliane when she was just a young babe."

"She's still a babe," Rudy said.

"Oof," Liliane said. "Enough of that."

The piano player had started again. He had a way of approaching the keyboard as if the motion of his own hands surprised him. He was really the best thing she'd seen in New York.

"You love music, don't you?" the boy turned and said. "I could tell by the way you walk."

She had to laugh. "I'm walking very much in your city."

"You have to let me show you some things. My New York."

"It's better than anyone else's New York?"

"You'll see," he said.

Oh, she would? She liked this boy, but his self-assurance could get annoying. She went back to looking at the piano player. How weary and quietly jaunty these tunes were. The man had found a good way to be old, she thought.

"I'll show you great neighborhoods," the boy said. "And you can show me Paris sometime."

"She's a good guide." Barbara snickered.

When the music was over, they all got up to leave. The boy went out to help them get a taxi, on the busier corner a block away. "You're gleaming in the night," he said to her. "Your satin."

"Let's hope a cab sees it," Barbara said.

"You look like the moon," he said. He reached out and flicked one of her dangling pearl earrings. His fingertip grazed her neck. *What is he doing?* she thought.

And then he was waving wildly at a cab, which did pull over and stop. "Tell me the name of your hotel," he said to her, very fast, "and I'll call so we can make a time for our walk." She wasn't so glad to say the hotel's name but she did. And then he swooped down on her for a kiss on the cheek. His bristled face smelled of sweat and the oils in male skin, and he whispered, "I look forward to seeing you," as he held her in a hug that went on too long. She gave him an icy look when it was over, but he was shaking hands with Barbara by then. He told the cabdriver, "Take very good care of these ladies."

Liliane had never in her life been insulted by the fact of male attention. It had not always been welcome, but she had never held it against men that they were bothering her with their desire or admiration. That was the way of things, and it usually served her well. In the cab, with Barbara half asleep and the dark streets outside, she was affronted by that dramatic hug. If she were young, she would've just known he wanted to have sex with her (everyone did), but it was about money. He was trying to use her vanity for money.

And she didn't have that much money. The insult was for nothing. Was this how the Indian lepers were fed? When she got back to the hotel that night, she went to bed and dreamed that she was entirely naked and sitting on the gritty curb of a city street. She was trying to cover herself—she looked in the gutter for old plastic bags and wrappers, dirty pages of newspaper, and she held these scraps of garbage against her lap. And there were naked children, a whole row of them, settled in the street alongside her, foraging refuse the same way. The children called her "madame," they were saying something to her, but then she woke up.

She was under clean white sheets in her hotel in New York and the room was cold. Americans liked air-conditioning too much. There was no reason for her to be here. What did she want from this place? Recreation, diversion, escape. This rough, crude city, full of grasping morons: What had she been thinking?

The next day, which was Sunday, Rudy felt the effects of last night's alcohol, but he did remember that he had to call Deedee before he did anything else. She was a person who actually went to church, so he lingered over breakfast until noon, and then she answered her home phone. "I wanted to ask you about Liliane," he said. "Donors always want things. You know, kinds of satisfaction. What would she want?"

"You know what I worry about," Deedee said. "If she's a Muslim—which of course is perfectly fine—we fund all these centers for Hindus. You can see in the photos they have statues of gods with garlands of marigolds on them in the courtyards. She might not like that. Lot of violence between the groups in India."

Oh, please. Deedee was usually a little sharper than that.

"Do you think she might want to dedicate something as a gift for her husband?" he said.

"What a lovely idea," Deedee said. "I never thought of that. That's how you do what you do, isn't it? You can think of how people can do the right thing and please themselves too."

"Yes, well, there's always a challenge in getting some romance into leprosy."

"I know there are romantic stories," Deedee said. "You wrote them."

It was true that in the last newsletter Rudy had written a feature about Bamala and Pandi, two infected people in a center near Thanjavur. They had been engaged to each other as children in a village, but then the engagement was broken when Bamala became sick. Years later they met by chance at a Hansen's Hope center when Pandi was very ill. He was now doing well on drugs, Bamala had grown older and stronger, and they were planning to marry.

And how was Rudy going to work that into a conversation? And there were parts left out—damage, abandonment, trauma, ostracism. But he liked the story, and who didn't like it when love triumphed? Rudy was not himself a fool for love. He had resisted Berry, in India, surely the woman he'd loved best, when she wanted him to settle with her for good. Why had he not leaped at that chance? Well, he hadn't.

He thought Liliane, who was not likely to get any other husbands at this stage, might go for the idea of a handsome memorial gesture, a Taj Mahal. It was, frankly, the only thing he could think of.

Rudy had dealt with any number of widows. You had to tread very carefully, not to kick against any anguished regrets or buried anger. You had to keep remembrances abstract. No frankness. Once, at a funeral, he'd heard the dead person's best friend say, "She was such a fucking prima donna." This was said right in the eulogy, and the dead person had once been Rudy's girlfriend, not too long before. It was Clara, the girl who'd told him what a high-stress job he had.

How hard he had been on Clara, with her pop-psych sympathy for one well-fed white man's office job. He'd told her she had no clue, and she'd said, "No one can talk to you, you're such a snob, you think you've visited hell like Jesus." But she had been weeping as she said it, he was more or less out the door. And a few months later she had died, from the mistake of walking into an unmarked elevator shaft, before she could learn anything.

He was sorry that he hadn't seen fit to be nicer to her; the dead can get you that way. He let women go too easily (a number of women had mentioned this), and he did act as if he were the only person in the so-called first world untainted by privilege. Liliane could probably tell this about him already.

So this was the plan. Rudy would take Liliane on a fascinating excursion, nothing too exhausting, and then Deedee would join them for a pleasant, cozy cocktail in the late afternoon. He called Liliane at her hotel and told her they were going to skip the obvious spots and get into real neighborhoods instead.

"I'm not sure," Liliane said. "Can I call you later?"

He was depressed when he hung up. What else did she have to do? He'd had in mind Jackson Heights, in Queens, which had as many South Asians as Mumbai, or was that an urban myth? Rolled leaves of *beeda* and beaded saris in the store windows. The Patel Brothers Supermarket, bins of okra and bitter gourds and pomelos, sacks of rice in three dozen varieties, rosewood rolling pins, round brass thali trays. Would she like that? An India of plenty—maybe that was the wrong message. No, she would like it.

Or maybe a Moroccan neighborhood? Her husband was Moroccan. There was a teeny area in Astoria, there was a restaurant people liked.

Or maybe she would like to see where he grew up. Rudy had lived his first eighteen years in an East Village apartment his parents had cleverly subdivided, with a room for him with his own "treehouse," aka a loft bed. His parents both worked for a left-leaning radio station—they were a stormy couple and were enchanted but neglectful parents. In his teen years his mother had begun to die, slowly and fitfully, from leukemia, and he and his father had cooked for her and played her favorite music all day and night, Otis Redding and John Lennon and Country Joe and the Fish. Now Rudy's father lived upstate, with a new wife, but the old neighborhood on Second Avenue was not all that changed.

He would give Liliane a day or two, he didn't pressure people. What if she said no? Either she would or she wouldn't. What were the chances of her ever giving a penny to Hansen's Hope? He'd say thirty percent. Sometimes he still thought like an investment banker. It would help his case to know more about the husband. She used her own last name, so the man couldn't be Googled. And how many Moroccan sheikhs were there? A search brought up religious leaders, which could not be right.

It was ridiculous that the roof of a building that housed sick children in Tamil Nadu was still leaking because he hadn't coaxed the funds out of a bored and overdressed old woman. He hated the way the world was set up, and he was sorry nobody wanted to overthrow these people anymore. He was sorry he couldn't just squash her flat and drain all the money out of her, he really was.

Rudy was not in the best mood when he went out that night. He spent too many hours in a bar on Rivington Street, where he kept having one more beer to get over being pissed off (famous fallacies of the already-drunk) and he got into a conversation with some lunkhead who was holding forth about the Ground Zero Mosque, did it *have* to be in *that* spot, and who really, really was paying for it?

"It's called Park51," Rudy said. "That's its name."

"That's what the Muslims call it," the guy said. "You don't happen to be a Muslim, do you? By any chance?"

Rudy thought of Liliane and was sorry she had to see his city at this particular inglorious moment. "I'm the rich terrorist who's pouring all my piles of gold into the project," Rudy said. "Can't you tell?"

"Very funny," the guy said.

"I'm a riot," Rudy said. And then he got up and left, lunkishly.

He thought, as he walked to the subway, that Liliane must find it complicated to be, essentially, a Muslim in disguise. If her wedding was in a mosque, she had to have converted. He knew that much. And then the woman had flown three and half thousand miles all the way to New Fucking York to hear the bigoted crap you heard on every corner now.

Liliane was cheered by one thing in New York, the prices were very good here. Not all the styles in shop windows were that nice, but she had learned to find her way through Bloomingdale's and had picked up a perfect sundress and some wonderful voile shirts she bought in three colors. Her euros went far, and just because she'd lost money didn't mean she didn't have *any*. What to get for her son, Emile? He was remarkably indifferent to clothes. Ahmed was the only one who'd ever bought him anything he liked. He still wore an ancient, stretched-out alpaca turtleneck his stepfather had given him. Ahmed himself had a tendency to give away whatever you gifted him with. Liliane had seen a drummer onstage in the club wearing an Armani sports jacket she'd bought Ahmed for his birthday. Ahmed managed to not let her or anyone be insulted either—he was so jolly and righteous and certain.

Bloomingdale's had absolutely nothing that Emile would like, but she bought herself a very pretty cuff bracelet, chunks of coral and turquoise set in brass. It cost more than she meant to pay, and once she had it in her shopping bag, she was cranky and morose and regretful. She kept it anyway, as if she were defying herself.

Later, before she went to bed, Liliane was very happy to see a text message on her phone from her son. The cheeses were going well, which meant he was selling enough so they didn't all go bad. Emile's ambitions were modest. He had a boyfriend who was an architect, not getting much work these days, but they didn't live together, and Emile seemed to feel no pressure to earn more and be richer.

Liliane had always wanted to be richer, though she had stopped being a gold digger after a certain point. When was that point? It was after she ran off with cash from the American clarinet player, and it was not because she felt bad about him. What did he need money for? Just to drink himself to ruin.

How terrific she had looked then, in the clothes that were chic enough to get a better catch. The catch she drew was an affectionate and generous man in his forties, who was a vice president of Carrefour and was divorced from a much dumpier woman. He seemed delighted to be with someone like Liliane, beautiful and full of fun, and he was not the worst lover either. But he was used to certain habits of command. He liked to summon her to come to him at two in the morning, he liked to tell her what to wear when they went out, and he fell into a vile, ugly outburst in a taxi once after she'd disagreed with him in front of his friends. "Inequities of wealth erode civility," her friend Yvette, who was a Marxist, said. To suffer indignities from a man you were crazy about was not unusual, even for Liliane, but to be maltreated by someone you didn't love was degrading. She had expected much more triumph in the arrangement, which, in the end, did not suit her at all.

And so she had gone from one barely solvent boyfriend to another, until the big surprise of her pregnancy, but at least she'd liked these men. She hadn't known she was any sort of purist, but it turned out she was.

• • •

Rudy waited for Liliane to call the next day, and she didn't. *She doesn't hate you,* he reminded himself, but maybe she did. He remembered a very odd look on her face when he hugged her good night. *Oh, fuck,* he thought—didn't he know better than to go around hugging Muslim women? What was the matter with him? He'd been to Malaysia, Sumatra, and north India, where you didn't even shake *hands*—what was the matter with him?

But the next morning, he wasn't in his office for five minutes before Veena, his assistant, told him Liliane was on the phone. "You must to show me the real city, not only the expensive parts," Liliane said.

"At your service," he said. "Ready when you are."

"The real city," she said.

What does a person want most? Rudy had been trained to think about that when cultivating prospects. He thought that Liliane, who always looked so beautifully put together, so effortlessly splendid for her age, probably wanted admiration. Nobody wears satin pants and mascara just for herself. He could bring some guy friends with him, just to hover around her, but that would make the outing less official, and he had only so much time to make his pitch while she was here. What a weird profession. At his jobs for colleges, he'd helped make "gift charts" in pyramids of how many donations they needed in various sizes, but HH was more of a by-the-seat-of-your-pants operation. His research on Liliane's assets had only shown a small French firm that moved property around, in a somewhat hyperactive way, and he was pretty sure there was more than that. The bad news was that there was no record of her giving big bucks—big euros—to any charity. Perhaps he would be her first. The one you never forget.

He didn't even believe in charities. What people needed was justice, not handouts. He'd been raised by Leftists, he knew all that. But death was catching up with the lepers before India had enough free health care. Nothing could stop death, but coins could be thrown back at him to slow him down.

In Rudy's club days as a teenager, he'd dated a girl who loved to come out of some venue at five in the morning, all spangled and sweaty and disheveled, and leave a twenty-dollar bill on the ground, for anyone on the street at that hour to find. It was something she liked to do before she went home, she thought it was lucky. Rudy, whose mother was starting to get sicker at this time, thought the girl didn't know a fucking thing about luck, but then he started leaving bits of money too. He'd tuck it in a subway grating or a sidewalk crack, a five or a ten, and hear himself think to it, *Please*.

A modern NGO did not beg for donations by claiming they would bring luck, though all over the world people left offerings around statues for luck. He'd heard Deedee talk about "blessings," but surely she knew not to say that to Liliane. It would not be good to get Liliane laughing in the wrong way.

Rudy had been thinking of Coney Island for their outing— funky, colorful, not too dangerous anymore—and was looking up its attractions on the computer at his desk at HH when Veena buzzed to tell him that Liliane was here—right here, now—in the office. This was a very good sign. Donors liked to think they owned the place, that it was theirs to pop in on.

But she was apologizing even as Veena showed her in. "You will think I am terrible," she said. She was canceling their outing, to go instead to some country house upstate with her friend Barbara.

Surely she would stay for a minute and have a nice cool glass of iced tea?

Well, she might just do that.

"That's so good, I need a break," he said. "I'm getting grief from one of the centers about their roof that never gets fixed."

"Yes, well, a roof."

"I'd love to see the place fixed because a couple is going to get married there soon. Bamala and Pandi. They were engaged as children but then Bamala was thrown out of the village when she came down with leprosy. Years later they met again, by chance. It's a great story."

Didn't he used to be better at this?

"It's like a story out of a Bollywood movie," he said. "Love lost and found."

He showed her their pictures on the computer. Pandi had a mustache and wore a white short-sleeved shirt over a wrapped plaid dhoti, and both he and Bamala, in her flowered cotton sari, were glowering into the camera.

"What is the church behind them?" Liliane asked.

"This center is run by a Congregationalist mission. They're a very dedicated bunch, very hardworking. People can do the right thing for whatever reasons they want. That's what I think. You know what I mean?"

She appeared not to. Veena brought in the tea then—what the hell had taken her so long?—and Rudy was grateful for a pause, while he figured out another route.

He was getting nowhere fast. The last time he had felt this bungling was in India, where he got things wrong all the time. What did he know about money? How had he managed to pick jobs where he had to count it and watch it? Maybe his idiocy was not to adore it enough. Maybe he had to be punished for lack of devotion to the force that ran the world.

Liliane hated the iced tea, full of sugar and ice cubes.

"Did you ever go to Morocco, with your husband?" Rudy said. "Is that where you were married?"

"We had a very splendid wedding," Liliane said. "I was carried into the room sitting on a cushioned table. Gold jewelry all around the face and, you know, henna designs on the hands and feet. My husband was on the shoulders of his friends. And wonderful music, long trumpets and much drums."

One of his cousins had had a wedding like that. She'd seen the videos at his sister's. Could anyone imagine her in a getup like that?

"Bamala and Pandi would be happy to just have a roof that didn't leak."

"Yes, of course."

"We lost a few of our donors last year because they'd had money invested with Madoff."

"What a liar he was," Liliane said. "A grand liar. Maybe he enjoyed to lie."

"I'd love to see someone give a gift in a spouse's memory, like the Shah Jahan gave the Taj Mahal for his Mumtaz. It would be an act of love."

What does he know about love? Liliane thought, in secret fury. *He has no idea whatsoever.*

She was thinking of the two times she had suffered most for love. One was when Emile was two weeks old. He would not let her sleep, not for a single second, and she was alone and broke and helpless in a hideous new way. The man who'd fathered him had run off with a girl from Frankfurt before Liliane had even known she was pregnant. A friend who showed up with some nice hot food thought Liliane should maybe think of giving the baby up to the care of the state, and Liliane had spit at her. Quick as that: a sudden spewed froth of saliva that hit her in the cheek. What a dramatic thing to do, and it lost her that useful friend. An act of love.

The other time had to do with Ahmed. Once, when they were first living together, she was sure he was still seeing another woman. Someone left over from before, a woman who sang sometimes at the club. He would come home in the early hours of the morning, he would decide he had to shower before he settled into bed, he would fix her a very lovely lunch the next day. She was afraid if she raged at him he would feel compelled to leave, and so she kept silent, she said nothing—she lived in a hell of patience, unlike anything she'd known, until he gave the woman up.

She could still remember his body in bed damp from the shower, his wet head on the pillow. Her silence was a sign (to her: there was no one else to see) that she was humbled, by this time, from the hard years. She could have found another man but not another Ahmed.

He used to bring home leftover food from the club to stretch their budget. Emile was a big eater. When had he started to have money? Not then. But he'd never been stingy. He'd had the club owner's love of grand gestures, buying champagne when the musicians' wives showed up, sending cribs and strollers to their new babies. Anyone could get a handout from him.

But he had hoarded those real estate properties, salted away his hidden riches. He must have loved to think of those assets growing in the dark, buried like bulbs till their season. When did he ever plan to tell her? Now she was rich because of him, which she sometimes forgot, thinking *like a rich person* that she had what she had from being worthy.

In her poorer days she'd been wily when she had to be. With nothing to eat in the house, she used to walk through elegant neighborhoods with her good haircut and good coat, and some perfectly decent men bought her meals. She was young and took chances. But she never sat down with anyone dangerous, she always knew how to judge, she had never been stupid or reckless.

"And older donors sometimes leave bequests in their wills," Rudy said. "That's another beautiful gesture."

What? She could hardly believe he'd decided to say this to her. How fast did he think she was on her way to dying?

"When people come to visit the Taj," Liliane said, "they don't want to see the poor people?"

He looked confused.

"In France I give to the homeless."

"On the street. Me too."

"No, no," she said. "Not little coins. I am a major donor to a fund we have that helps the homeless musicians, you know, the ones who play and beg. Some of them are very good!"

"That's wonderful of you."

"I have given to them more than I ought to. Nothing left. I'm glad."

"Many of our lepers," Rudy said, "are found living on the streets. Well, I can't call them *our* lepers."

"They're yours, not mine!" she said, laughing.

"All our cities," he said, "are full of suffering. New York too."

"I very much am looking forward," she said, "to getting out now to the countryside. The mountains are cooler, yes? It will be peaceful."

"You'll have a great time with your friends, I know," he said. "We'll miss you, but I wouldn't want to keep you from going."

He'd given up, she could tell. He knew when defeat had arrived. He pushed back his hair and rubbed his eyes, as if he were already alone.

But that was not the end of the story. Liliane realized she'd better say goodbye, since she probably wasn't going to see Rudy again before she went back to Paris. It actually had been a pleasure, hadn't it, despite his having made an imbecile of himself trying this way and that to work her. She thought she might leave just a token donation, out of politeness, and because she was not heartless.

Rudy said, "You know, maybe Bamala will have henna on her hands for her wedding like you did. They do that in India too."

Could he not stop? But Liliane found herself holding out

her own hands, as if a design were on them. As a child, she'd had to hold them like that when her father smacked them with a belt buckle to punish her, but that was another story. One probably familiar to this Bamala. Human life had always been atrocious; no one had to tell Liliane that.

"I hope her wedding day is as beautiful as mine was," Liliane said.

Ahmed had always said he hated the stinginess of the French. When Liliane left the office, she had signed away fifteen thousand dollars on her credit card. Quite a heady sensation, she noticed. She hadn't known she was going to do that. Rudy had probably hoped for much more—who knew what most of those donors gave?—but his face had been very tender with thanks and he had said it would greatly help one badly leaking roof.

"People will be dry there this fall," he said. "*Insha'Allah.*"

On the way back to the hotel she was really in quite a wonderful frame of mind. As if she had just been on a great shopping spree. Which she had. She couldn't wait to tell Emile, who always accused her (silently and otherwise) of being shallow.

Later she wondered if she had made a mistake. She'd come to New York to forget how much money she'd lost, and she had just managed to dole out another wad. She felt preposterous, an old puppet of comic twists. He had been dogged with her, in his nice-boy way, and then she had turned around and surprised him. Which she still knew how to do. She had known how to wait before she caught him off guard.

What an odd story she had to tell, when she got back to Paris: she'd come all this way to drop a bundle of money on poor people in South Asia. People she'd never met! She'd never done such a thing in her life. Never too late! She could tell the story in a way that didn't make her look entirely foolish. Or she could keep it to herself.

Now she was a friend to lepers: she was getting used to the idea, she liked it. So this was the end to her time in New York, an ugly and interesting city. *Une histoire qui finit bien.* Rudy, that awkward boy, was probably being congratulated by the staff in his office. Maybe they were toasting her with little plastic cups. To Liliane! She hoped he was leading the toast. Despite the rudeness of his not having hugged her goodbye this time.

She wanted to tell Ahmed what she had done. He would have thought well of her for it, would have gotten that look of beaming pleasure on his face—he tended to applaud people who acted rashly out of their better natures. He liked nothing better than that, and would not have allowed anyone to see anything ridiculous in what she'd just done. And who would, who in the world? She had never in her life been someone people laughed at.